WHISPERS OF HOLIDAY MAGIC IN SWEETWATER SPRINGS

JOSIE RIVIERA

PRAISE AND AWARDS

USA TODAY bestselling author

INTRODUCTION

To keep up on newly released ebooks, paperbacks, Large Print Paperbacks, audiobooks, as well as exclusive sales, sign up for Josie's Newsletter today.

As a thank you, I'll send you a Free PDF ... The Beauty Of ...

Josie's Newsletter

Did you know that according to a Yale University study, people who read books live longer?

This book is dedicated to all my wonderful readers who have supported me every inch of the way.
THANK YOU!

ACKNOWLEDGMENTS

An appreciative thank you to my patient husband, Dave, and our three wonderful children.

CHAPTER 1

The first snowflakes of winter drifted lazily past the frost-etched windows of *Blissful Bites*. Inside, miniature white bulbs shimmered against garlands of pine, their cheery sparkle at odds with the chaos that had overtaken Emma Jacobsen's once-pristine bakery.

Where neat displays of artisanal breads and delicate pastries once reigned, now teetered precarious stacks of cardboard boxes. Tinsel and ornaments spilled from overstuffed bins, mingling with piles of age-stained periodicals and battered recipe collections. Spicy fragrances of the holidays—gingerbread and cinnamon sticks—blended with the dusty breath of abandoned keepsakes.

Emma stood in the eye of the storm, her white apron streaked with flour, her hair coming loose from its once neat ponytail. The frustration of another day where nothing had gone right tugged at her heart. An old recipe card, her mother's handwriting scarcely legible, rested beneath her palm as if waiting for her to resurrect it.

She wanted to. Oh, how she wanted to.

But something inside her had shifted—ever since

Theodore and Lillian Weatherly's wedding two years ago. It was as though she'd been frozen in place.

The piles in the shop seemed to grow in direct proportion to the memories she clung to, suffocating the part of her that used to take joy in the simplest of holiday traditions. A cascade of mismatched teacups rattled as she tugged on a drawer, narrowly avoiding disaster.

"Clumsy me," she muttered, though the truth ran deeper than her fumbling hands.

Her gaze landed on a postcard tucked between cookbooks.

Venice's canals glimmered in the photo, in vivid opposition to Sweetwater Springs, her hometown and its cobblestone streets. Victor's note promised, "Someday we'll see this together." That was before he had vanished, leaving her with nothing but a hollow "It's complicated" and unanswered calls.

Outside, Sweetwater Springs sparkled. Storefronts along Main Street dazzled with seasonal splendor, and wreaths and holly framed the doorways. A damp chill clung to the air, heavy with the earthy scent of rain-soaked fir needles. Moss-covered branches drooped, occasional plops of slush hitting the ground. Nearby, the muffled voices of bundled-up neighbors mingled with the squeak of rubber boots on wet pavement.

It was the first week of December, and, in the town square, a towering evergreen rose ready for the annual tree-lighting ceremony. On the sidewalks, townsfolk huddled together, exchanging bright smiles and animated plans.

A group of carolers in Victorian costumes sang a nostalgic version of *Silent Night*, their voices drifting through the air like a forgotten lullaby. Inside, the quiet of the bakery amplified the weight pressing against Emma's chest.

She stared at the trays of untouched cookie dough, abandoned when the effort of simply stirring the batter had become too much. The mixing bowl mocked her, a monument to her paralysis. Once, she'd whipped up batches of cookies without a second thought. Now, each ingredient weighed a ton, laden with memories of happier times. She longed to recapture that spark, but fear of disappointment kept her rooted in place.

Her gaze flickered to a framed photo of Theodore and Lillian Weatherly that sat among a jumble of cake stands. The couple looked so happy—reunited in their seventies, having found love after all those years apart. Emma had been overjoyed for them, but that joy came with a cost, one she hadn't expected. Their happiness had heightened the absence of her parents, reopening wounds she'd tried to bury.

She wiped a tear from her cheek, reminding herself not to cry. Not anymore.

She remained motionless in her quiet sanctuary, a realm apart from the bustling outside world. The joyous preparations that had once filled her days—crafting gingerbread houses, piping translucent sugar snowflakes—were overwhelming. How was it possible to create when the surfaces of her shop were so cluttered?

Upholding her parents' legacy seemed unattainable as the bakery slipped from her grasp.

Every recipe that didn't turn out right, every less-than-perfect day—was a reminder that she was failing. The idea of moving anything, of altering the traditions her parents had cherished, filled her with dread. She wondered if it was her refusal to let go that was holding her captive.

Her mind drifted back to the moments that had upended her world. It wasn't only Theodore and Lillian's wedding that had triggered her hoarding—it was the realization that came with it. As she'd watched them exchange vows, a truth she'd avoided for years had finally sunk in: the loved ones in her life, all of them, were never returning.

Years earlier, her mother's unexpected death in a car accident had left her reeling. Her father had passed away from a sudden heart attack a few years before. Somehow, she'd clung to the irrational hope that it was all a mistake and they'd walk through the bakery door any day.

At present, the upcoming Holiday Market fundraiser loomed large. It was more than festive cheer; the town's future hung in the balance. Without the funds for a new community center, Sweetwater Springs risked losing its charm to encroaching chain stores. Emma's contribution of baked goods would help the project, but her kitchen remained stubbornly silent.

Observing Theodore, who had played the role of a grandfather, begin a new phase had tipped the scales and completely shattered her fragile illusions.

She understood, on some level, that surrounding herself with more stuff wouldn't bring anyone back or stop time from ticking. However, the thought of casting aside even one item and facing a future without these tangible reminders of security paralyzed her. It was easier to hide among the memories, to pretend that if she held onto these things, she wasn't ever alone.

As Emma sank deeper into her thoughts, reality intruded with a sharp rap on the front window. The sound jolted her from her reverie, a clear reminder that the world outside continued to turn despite her internal struggles.

Through the fogged glass, Nora Fitzwater's concerned face peered in, the town librarian forever fussing over her friends.

Nevertheless, Emma was incapable of allowing Nora entry, not today—not when the bakery was in such disarray.

Instead, she pointed to the CLOSED sign, mouthing an apology as Nora reluctantly retreated.

Emma slumped against the counter, letting her body slide to the floor, her back pressed to the cool wood of the cabinets. The ticking of the clock on the wall echoed her heartbeat, both too fast and too loud. She rested her head on her knees, trying to resist the wave of hopelessness threatening to drag her under.

As she sat there, her gaze fell on a dusty box tucked beneath the counter. Curiosity sparked, and she pulled it out. Among old receipts and faded photographs was a small, sepia-toned image. She squinted, making out the silhouette of a lighthouse against a stormy sky. She flipped it over, her heart skipping at the words: *The beacon that guards our secrets - 1852.*

She'd never seen this photo before, and the date made little sense. They didn't build the lighthouse until years later.

Outside, bells jingled—a sleigh ride or perhaps someone with harness bells walking past the bakery. She ignored it until a shadow moved past the front window. A man, tall and broad-shouldered, with the kind of presence that made her heart skip. Strong jaw, aquiline nose, and dark eyes that seemed to take in everything at once.

He moved with an odd grace, despite the slight limp that interrupted his stride. His dark wool coat flapped open in the wind, and a briefcase swung from one hand as he paused, studying her storefront.

She blinked, her pulse quickening. Surely he wasn't wearing a fedora.

But no, he wasn't.

He was a stranger. Wait. Could it be? Her heart gave a sharp twist as recognition bloomed. Victor Steele. She hadn't seen him in … not since …

Her thoughts scattered. The door was locked, though for

a breathless moment, she feared he'd try it anyway. He paused, his gaze sweeping over the CLOSED sign with a shake of his head before continuing down the street.

Why had he returned? And why now, when she was barely holding it together?

Her hands trembled as she pushed herself up, peering through the binoculars she'd left by the window, her curiosity overriding her better judgment. Now he stood beneath the enormous Christmas tree, his head tilted back. Then he shrugged, as if clearing away some stray thought.

Victor continued, walking toward the Sweetwater Inn, but his arrival had stirred something in her, something she believed she had buried.

She wasn't sure what scared her more—the mess in her life or the way her heart had leaped at the sight of him.

The logical thing would be to phone Olivia Whitfield, owner of *Harper's Haven*, the adjacent bookshop, to ask if she saw the man. However, that meant admitting that Emma had been hiding, avoiding their concerned overtures.

Her reflection in the smudged oven door exposed what she feared. Her blond hair tangled into a mess, and exhaustion shadowed her blue eyes.

Her gaze fell on a half-finished batch of her celebrated cranberry-orange muffins, the batter thick and unbaked, abandoned earlier when the very idea of baking became too overwhelming. An almost forgotten spark flickered. Memories of laughter, of comradery shared with others, and the fulfillment of creating sweet desserts that brought happiness to people.

Perhaps … perhaps it was time to step out of the shadows. To reconnect with the town she cherished, to verify the identity of the man who had stirred a quickening in her heart she couldn't ignore.

With a determined breath, she resolved to finish the

muffins. As the aroma filled the air an hour later, she dared to imagine what possibilities tomorrow might hold.

THE NEXT MORNING, Emma stood at her bedroom window, the early light of dawn casting shadows over the town's preparations for the Holiday Market. Volunteers bustled on the cobblestone streets below, setting up booths with light-hearted conversation. The sounds seemed foreign in her quiet world of flour-dusted counters and half-finished pastries.

She reminded herself of her long-standing commitment to supply baked goods for the event. For years, her signature treats—crisp peppermint bark and snickerdoodles—had been the first to vanish from the tables.

Minutes later, she emerged from the shower. She slipped a tailored apron over a bright-red sweater embroidered with snowflake patterns. The apron, cinched at the waist, boasted a cheerful gingham print that lifted her spirits. She paired it with comfortable, dark-wash jeans and slip-resistant clogs.

She ran her fingers over her grandmother's bracelet, the cool metal pressing reassurance into her skin. She was capable. She *had* to do this.

With a deep breath, Emma descended the stairs into the bakery. Boxes teetered, bins overflowed, and somewhere beneath it all was the Emma Jacobsen who once baked with joy. Today, she would find that woman again—even if it meant starting small.

She picked up a whisk, its recognizable weight both comforting and challenging.

"Come on, Emma," she whispered. "It's just baking."

Her hand fell on a recipe card. Her grandmother's handwriting detailed the secret to creating perfect snickerdoodles.

Brown butter.

Brown butter added depth and richness to the cookies. Cooking butter until the milk solids caramelized gave the butter a nutty, toasty flavor.

The clock on the wall ticked relentlessly, reminding Emma of her commitment to the Holiday Market. She should be measuring flour, creaming butter and sugar, and filling the shop with the bolstering scents of cinnamon and vanilla.

With shaking hands, she reached for a notepad. She started writing, hesitantly at first, then with growing determination:

Clear one counter.

Bake one batch of snickerdoodles.

Attend Market for 30 minutes.

Not much, though it was a beginning. As she wrote, an ornament rolled across the floor, coming to rest at her feet. A delicate glass snow globe, and inside, a tiny scene of Sweetwater Springs in winter. Emma picked it up and shook it, marveling at how it captured the holiday essence of her beloved town.

For the first time in months, hope glimmered. Perhaps, like this snow globe, she could create a manageable world within the chaos. A space where she could reconnect with her passion for baking, with her friends, and possibly even herself.

The calming rhythm of measuring and mixing beckoned. She squinted at the recipe card, although she knew the ingredients by heart.

A knock sounded at the back door. "The door's open," she called without looking up, expecting a delivery of fresh cranberries from the local farm for her holiday tarts.

"Still burning the midnight oil, I see." The voice was deep, familiar—with a tinge of a French accent.

Her heart stumbled in her chest. Slowly, she turned.

Victor Steele filled the doorway. The wind had tousled his dark hair, and a few days' worth of stubble shadowed his jaw. Specks of snow clung to his boots. His piercing dark eyes sparkled with amusement and something more. The kind of *something* that had once awakened her heart.

The measuring cup slipped from her fingers, clattering to the floor.

"Victor," she breathed, admonishing herself to recover her composure quickly. "Midnight oil? It's nine o'clock in the morning. Many of us start our days before noon."

He pointed to himself. "And me?"

"Not so much."

He chuckled, the rich sound sending an involuntary quiver along her spine. "I see your wit is as sharp as ever," he replied.

"I assumed you were still in Venice. I haven't heard from you in a long time." She bent to pick up her measuring cup while having the beneficial effect of avoiding his stare.

"I've been traveling. Sometimes, it's difficult to connect."

"Even in this modern day with the use of cell phones and the internet?"

"Emma, for that, I am sorry." The scent of him—a hint of cedar and spice—stirred memories she had tried hard to suppress. It was almost unfair how easily his presence brought those memories rushing back, unraveling the careful walls she'd built.

She stood, glanced at him, then down at the counter.

Their relationship had been brief. Victor had been in town for a few months before he'd abruptly left after receiving a substantial inheritance.

During that short time, they'd developed a connection both exciting and terrifying. She'd welcomed his visits to the bakery, their conversations flowing easily from local gossip to thought-provoking discussions. Theirs was a friendship that might've deepened into something more. At least, that was what she'd hoped.

But when he left, the hollowness that ensued was more profound than she had expected. She wondered if she'd imagined their entire connection.

"Welcome back," she managed, inwardly chastising herself for her lack of anything more brilliant to say. "I'm guessing this isn't a social call?"

"It is, but there's more. I was informed about some financial trouble," he said. "Elliot is occupied with related legal matters, so he requested my assistance."

Elliot Fitzwater had married Nora. Elliot was related to Victor, and the men's physical resemblance to each other was astounding.

"Trouble? What kind of trouble?" Emma asked, trying to focus on the present, not on the months of silence and the what-ifs that flooded her mind.

Victor closed the gap between them. His limp was slight, but still there. He'd told her he had had a sports injury when he was young. Soccer. He'd landed on the field and tore a ligament. "My professional athletic career ended before it began," he'd said matter-of-factly.

In times past, he'd shared many a good story with her, and with each hour, she'd fallen in love with him a little more. Those long afternoons returned in vivid detail. The jokes. The way his eyes lit up when they talked about the future. The way her heart had stuttered with possibility.

"All kinds of trouble," he was saying, snapping her back to the present. "Elliot figured that my expertise in finance might be useful in sorting it out."

She wiped her damp palms on her apron. She was acutely aware of a flour smudge on her cheek and her messy hair. Of course, Victor would show up now, unfairly handsome, when she was at her most disheveled. Fortunately, at least she had showered.

"You? Why?" she questioned. "There are several excellent accountants in town."

His expression was somber, but his eyes—those piercing dark eyes that had haunted her dreams for months—held a heat that warmed her cheeks.

"As I explained, because Elliot asked for my help," he said. "We've been in touch."

"Lately?" she inquired, bitterness edging her voice despite herself.

"Off and on."

Yet he couldn't take the time to be in touch with her, Emma thought, the familiar pang of hurt rising.

"The town is planning to expand the pediatric wing at Sweetwater Springs General, and Elliot is spearheading the project," Victor continued.

"I'm well aware. Nora has spoken of little else for months. Some of the money will go toward a new community center." She reached up to adjust the loose strands of hair that had slipped from her ponytail. A quick glance in the kitchen mirror confirmed she had flour smudges on her cheeks. Both cheeks. Typical. She scrubbed the flour away with a paper towel, the embarrassment heating her face.

"You mentioned trouble?" she inquired, hoping to steer the conversation away from becoming too personal.

"Donations that were unaccounted for and allegations of embezzlement," he replied. "The town is in a panic. If we can't sort this out—"

"We?"

"I'm part of this community, too, Emma."

She crossed her arms defensively. "Since when?"

Victor sighed, as though carefully choosing his next words. "Since now. I could use your help. You know this town and its people, better than I do. Frankly, I've missed your insight. And I missed you, Raindrop."

The old nickname caught her off guard, the tenderness in his tone wrapping around her. *Raindrop.* He'd named her that during one of their late-night conversations.

But now the word stung.

She shook her head. "Such an odd name."

"Is it? That's how I see you—unique and precious, because no two raindrops are alike."

A flutter stirred in her chest, one she tried desperately to push aside. She couldn't let herself feel the pull of his words again, not after everything.

"Honestly," she said, voicing only a portion of her inner turmoil, "I haven't been out much lately."

He nodded slightly, taking in the bakery's state—the flour-sprinkled counters, the half-empty sugar jar, the haunting sense of disarray. "This is important, and it might be good for you."

She hesitated, inclined to say no, though torn between the safety of seclusion and the attraction of Victor's appeal. Their shared history flashed through her mind—playful debates over the best film noir classics, the almost-kiss a few days before he left, the texting and phone calls once he'd settled in Europe. His absence had filled her with a void deeper than she had ever thought imaginable.

She'd debated if they should continue their correspondence, but he'd decided for her. He'd disappeared.

Now he'd reappeared, asking for her help as if that lengthy span of silence and the unanswered letters she'd sent him hadn't happened.

It had been easier, in a way, when he was in Venice –out of sight, if never quite out of mind. A part of her longed to say yes. To step backward, back into the easy rapport they once shared.

"I don't know," she said.

"C'mon, Emma. Us working together."

Us. Such a simple word, and yet it held so much potential, so much risk. Before she responded, a commotion outside drew them both to the front of the bakery.

They peered out the window. She recognized Nora's bright green coat and saw Elliot's animated gestures as he spoke to the sheriff. These were her friends. People she'd shared laughter and tears with.

She should be out there, mingling, bringing in customers for the bakery. However, the idea of confronting their probing questions was unbearable. Staying in the kitchen, lost in the comforting mess of her work, was simpler.

She kept telling herself it was about productivity, though she couldn't ignore the truth—she was avoiding it all.

"Let's see what's going on," Victor said.

Her gaze fell on a photograph pinned to the cluttered corkboard above her workspace. Her parents smiled back at her, flour-dusted and happy in front of the bakery on its opening day. What would they think of her now, hiding away from the world they'd loved being a part of?

She took a deep, shaky breath. The anxiety was still there, a tight knot in her stomach, but alongside it was a flicker of something else. Determination? Optimism?

"Okay," she whispered, more to herself than to Victor. Then, louder, "Okay."

He turned to her, one dark eyebrow raised. "While we're at it, are you up to a little detective work?"

"Let's see what we can do about this fundraiser first." Her voice didn't carry the strength of conviction, but at least the words were out there.

Victor's smile deepened, a soft curve at the edges. "You're still that brave woman I remember."

She felt the familiar tug at her heart, but she pushed it

aside and grabbed her coat. She couldn't afford to let herself get swept up in him again. "I'm not doing this for you, Victor. This is for the town."

"Of course," he said, his tone a little too understanding, a little too close for comfort.

He opened the door for her, gesturing to the street where the small crowd had gatered. "Shall we?"

As Emma stepped outside, the cool morning air nipped at her cheeks, bringing with it a flurry of smells—damp earth, fresh coffee from a nearby café, and the faint scent of pine on the breeze. The town was waking up around her, much like a part of herself that had been in hibernation.

Victor stood beside her, the warmth of his presence undeniable despite the coolness of the air.

"One careful step after another," she muttered.

"You say something?" he asked, glancing at her.

"Nothing. Let's go find out what's happening."

The two of them made their way across the street, and though her heart still held the heaviness of unresolved feelings and unanswered questions, she couldn't deny there was something stirring within her. A sense of purpose. Of connection.

Maybe it wasn't only the town she had to reconnect with. Maybe it was time to figure out how Victor fit into her life or if he ever would again.

First, she had a fundraiser to save. And possibly, a few ghosts from the past to lie to rest.

CHAPTER 2

*A*s Emma and Victor emerged into a raw pewter gray chill, the impact of Sweetwater Springs' festive transformation hit Emma's senses.

The familiarity of the town's traditions enclosed her like a cozy quilt, worn but still warm. The cobblestone streets, lined with tiny shops and century-old buildings, brimmed with holiday cheer. Children's laughter echoed through the air as they chased one another around the cherry blossom trees, their reddish-brown, skeletal branches creating a stark contrast against the snow.

When she and Victor first began seeing each other, the dream of planting a tree in the park as a symbol of their future together had floated through Emma's mind. It was a long-standing town tradition: when a man asked a woman to plant a tree with him: it was more than a gesture—it was a proposal of marriage. That dream had withered. It was hard to plant a tree with a guy who wasn't there.

She shook her head. No use in dwelling on what could have been.

"They're starting to set up for the Luminary Walk," Emma

murmured, nodding toward volunteers arranging lanterns along the paths. The walk was her parents' favorite tradition, held every Christmas Eve when townspeople would gather, light paper lanterns, and sing carols beneath the stars. She had once loved it too, before Theodore and Lillian began walking hand-in-hand, leaving her to watch from the sidelines.

In the heart of the square, the scent of Mrs. Harriet McAllister's hot chocolate floated through the air, rich and heady. The copper pot that rested over the fire, sending curls of steam skyward, was legendary in Sweetwater Springs. A cup of that cocoa thawed even the frostiest of hearts.

"Oh, look, the Giving Sleigh," Emma said, her tone brightening as they ducked into the historical society. Inside, a large sleigh, draped with ribbons and lights, sat ready for the community to fill with gifts for the less fortunate. By Christmas Eve, it would overflow with packages, a testament to the town's generosity.

"I'd almost forgotten how magical it all is." Emma scanned the square. "Even with what's happened, there's so much joy in this one little town."

"Never too late to be part of it again," Victor said, his deep voice sending a shiver through her. "The season is about fresh starts."

She glanced at him. "What was Christmas like for you growing up? A sleigh filled with presents, carols, and hot chocolate?"

He gave a rueful smile. "No tree, no lights, no Luminary Walk. It was just … another day. My family moved constantly."

She touched the sleek brass of the centennial plaque as they passed, outlining the date—1852. "Sweetwater Springs was far from picture-perfect," she said. "Legend has it, the town wasn't even supposed to be called Sweetwater."

"No?"

"According to my great-grandmother, the first settler, Jeremiah Sweet, won the land in a poker game. He bluffed his way to victory with nothing but a pair of twos, but convinced his opponent he had a royal flush. When asked to prove it, he said his hand was 'sweet as spring water.' The name stuck."

Victor chuckled. "That sounds about right. Every place has its secrets."

"Sweetwater has more than its fair share."

They continued down the lane, weaving through stalls being set up for the Holiday Market. Strings of red and green lights crisscrossed overhead, their glow casting a tint on the ground. The notes of *Silver Bells* drifted from the church tower, a reminder of all the decades Emma had spent listening to those chimes to mark the passing hours.

Victor's gaze roved over the square. "They've outdone themselves, haven't they?"

She nodded, nostalgia pulling at her heartstrings. She hadn't allowed herself to truly experience the magic of the season in a while. It was too risky, too painful. And yet, here she was, standing in the middle of it, allowing the memories to seep in.

As they walked, all the words that Emma had suppressed for months emerged. She painted a vivid picture of Sweetwater Springs' history—from the ill-fated attempt to breed racing ostriches in the 1930s to the time the entire community took part in a three-day game of hide-and-seek in 1967. An eccentric bunch of people, all living in one charming town," she summarized.

Victor smiled. "How do you know all this?"

"My parents were history buffs. We spent weekends interviewing the town elders. It was our thing."

Before she could lose herself in sentimentality, familiar voices called out to her.

"Emma! It's so good to see you," Nora said, sweeping her into a warm hug. "And Victor, welcome back. When did you get in?"

"Yesterday," he replied. "I expected Elliot would've mentioned it. After all, we are related."

"My husband?" Nora chuckled. "He's consumed by town business, and we hardly talk lately."

"Speaking of business …" Victor's expression became serious as he nodded to Elliot who had joined them. Elliot kissed his wife hello, then turned to Victor and Emma.

Victor gave a curt nod. "Anything new?"

"There are definitely discrepancies in the records going back years," Nora said. "Someone's been cooking the books for a while."

The air, which was filled with holiday cheer moments ago, now became brittle and tense.

Victor took charge, his tone calm but authoritative. "We need to go through every donation record for the past five years. Nora, can you assist? Elliot, we'll start with this year's pledges. And Emma …" He turned to her, his gaze softening. "Will you help me comb through the town hall archives? Two sets of eyes are better than one."

Her pulse quickened at the thought of working side by side with him. "Of course," she said.

As he issued instructions, Emma followed his every movement. Effortlessly, he coordinated the first stages of the investigation.

She smiled. This was the Victor she remembered—cool under pressure, always ready to refine a plan.

Elliot pulled off his felt brimmed hat and ran a hand through his hair. "I've mentioned for months that we need better oversight on the market committee. But no one wanted to 'mess with tradition'."

Olivia Whitfield, who owned the bookshop, *Harper's Haven*, next door to Emma's bakery, emerged to join them. "We've tried our best. The market is about community, not bureaucracy. Can we sort this out without involving outsiders? Consider the scandal, the consequences to the town's reputation."

"By outsiders, are you referring to me?" Victor asked.

"You're Elliot's relative, so you don't count."

Victor shrugged. "Thanks, I think."

"There's something else." Nora cleared her throat. "Gus Stratton, who is the treasurer at the historical society, cites irregularities in their accounts. Whatever's going on might be bigger than the Holiday Market."

Elliot broke the silence. "Perhaps Sweetwater Springs isn't as ideal as we like to think."

As they dispersed, Emma caught pieces of whispered conversations from the townspeople:

"Could be …?" "Absolutely not. They've been on the committee for years." "What if it goes all the way to the top?"

Young mothers huddled together, their bodies pressing in. "What about the children's hospital wing?" one fretted, bouncing a fussy infant on her hip.

When Emma and Victor continued past the square, a debate erupted between Mr. Granger, the bank manager, and Pete from the hardware store.

"It's city folk," Pete insisted, jabbing a finger at the sky. "Comin' in here with their fancy ideas."

"Oh, stuff it, Pete," Mr. Granger snapped.

"I'm staying here," Victor said, as he and Emma approached the Sweetwater Inn.

"The best accommodations in town."

Emma heard Mabel, the innkeeper, muttering to her

husband as they swept the expansive porch. "If word gets out about this scandal, there goes the tourist season. Might as well board up now."

Emma glanced at Victor. His slight nod told her he heard the conversation, too. Whatever happened with the Holiday Market money, unscrambling this mystery was far from straightforward. People were genuinely nervous.

Theodore and Lillian Weatherly walked toward them. Theodore's furrowed brow and tense expression mirrored the weight of the situation. Even Lillian, usually the picture of elegance, appeared rattled, her posture stiff and uncertain.

"How lovely to see you out and about," Lillian called out to Emma.

"Thanks. It's good to be here."

"We heard about the missing funds," Lillian said. "Can we do anything to help?"

"We're approaching the situation systematically," Victor replied. "Though we appreciate any insight."

"The founders hid important information in unexpected places, if that helps," Lillian said.

Before they all headed off, Emma's phone buzzed. She glanced at the screen, and her breath froze. A cryptic message from an unknown number: *Meet me at the old Peterson lumber camp. 9:30 PM.*

Her hand quivered as she deleted the message.

The Peterson lumber camp sat at the end of a twisting woodland road and was a ten-minute drive from town. Once an active operation, it currently existed as a ghostly reminder of the area's logging history. The clearing held remnants of bunkhouses, a mess hall, and the foreperson's cabin. When the timber industry declined, the camp's abandonment happened almost overnight, leaving behind rusting equipment and stories of unpaid wages and worker unrest. Despite its proximity to town, few ventured there, especially in the dark winter months, when shadows seemed to travel between the trees.

She hadn't set foot near that place in years.

Victor noticed her hesitation. "You okay?"

"Yeah, except ..." Emma forced a smile. "I need to check on a matter at the bakery. Will you be alright examining the town hall archives without me?"

"Yes, but are you sure?" His eyes searched hers, as if sensing something was off.

"I'll be fine," she insisted.

Victor hesitated, then nodded. "Alright. I'll be in touch."

As she walked away, Emma couldn't shake the sense that she was entering a situation that was far more dangerous than missing donations and gossip.

She forced air into her lungs and took a last look at Lillian and Theodore, their conversation fading into the background as she contemplated the cryptic text.

She hurried to the bakery, her thoughts reeling. Who could have sent it? And why meet at the lumber camp?

She glanced at her watch. 12:30 PM. She had several hours before the meeting. Part of her insisted she should notify Victor or the sheriff about the message, but another part—the part that craved answers and maybe a bit of adventure—urged her to go alone.

Already, she calculated the fastest route to the camp.

After all, weren't the town's founders known for their penchant for mystery?

CHAPTER 3

*B*ack at *Blissful Bites*, Emma paced the length of her bakery, her thoughts in disarray. The sensible thing to do would be to ignore the text and trust the official investigation. But as her gaze fell upon the photograph of her parents—their adventurous smiles frozen in time—a familiar spark ignited within her.

"*What would you do?*" she whispered to their smiling faces.

They would go. She knew it in her bones.

Hours later, she grabbed her hooded parka and a flashlight. She scribbled a brief note on a scrap of paper detailing where she'd gone and left it on the counter—just in case.

In case of what? The thought skittered through her mind.

She didn't dwell on that part, although she was intelligent enough to be safe.

Minutes later, she slipped out the back door and into the gathering twilight, the damp chill of the Pacific Northwest pressing in on her. She drove toward the old lumber camp, an ache of uncertainty gnawing at her. The anonymous text and the mention of the ledger had stirred something—a need to protect her town, to solve a mystery long buried. Yet with each passing mile, her logical mind screamed that this was reckless. Dangerous, even.

But she couldn't turn back now.

Her breath hitched as she veered left onto Cipher Lane, then took a sharp right down Riddle Row. *Of course*, she thought with a smile. The eccentric town founders had littered Sweetwater Springs with names like this. A community built by puzzle-loving intellectuals who'd hidden clues and ciphers in its very foundations. Her parents had loved the quirky history, though Emma was thinking "eccentric" was a mild term.

As she pulled into the clearing at 9:25 PM, her headlights flickered over the crumbling remains of the abandoned camp. Fog slithered between the decaying buildings, the oppressive silence stretching over her like a cloak. A shiver coursed through her—not from the cold, but from the eerie isolation.

What was she really doing out here?

However, it was too late to second-guess herself. She parked, grabbed her flashlight, and stepped into the frost-covered clearing. The earth crunched beneath her boots. Her light caught on a faded **NO TRESPASSING** sign, hanging crookedly from a rusty chain-link fence. Ignoring it, she pressed on.

"Hello?" Her voice sounded unnaturally small in the vast emptiness. "Anyone?" Silence. Only the low rustling of wind through barren branches.

She checked her watch—9:32 PM. Her breath clouded in the frosty night air as she stood at the threshold of the main building, debating whether to go inside or wait. A muffled thud from within made the decision for her. Inhaling sharply, she gripped the door handle and pushed it open; the hinges groaning in protest.

"I'm here," she called, sweeping her flashlight beam across the room. "I got your message."

As her vision adjusted to the dim light, a faint glow seeped from a distant corridor, barely illuminating the cracked and crumbling walls. With cautious steps, she edged closer, her senses hyper-aware of every creak.

At the end of the corridor, she peered around the corner and stopped. A single figure was hunched over a desk, illuminated by the flickering glow of a camping lantern. Her breath caught when she recognized him.

"Gus Stratton?" she gasped. "What on earth are you doing here?" The historical society's most senior—and most enigmatic—member looked up, his face worn and shadowed by the dim light. His eyes glinted with something unreadable.

"Emma. I wasn't sure you'd come."

"Gus, I—what is this?" She peered at every corner of the deserted room, tension coiling in her gut. "You scared me half to death. I didn't see your vehicle."

"My pickup truck is behind the mess hall, out of sight from the main road. I had to be discreet."

"Why all the intrigue?" Emma gestured vaguely. "You had the option to drop by my bakery rather than resorting to a mysterious text."

"Heard your place has been shuttered lately," Gus replied, his tone careful. "You seldom answer the door if anyone knocks."

Her jaw locked, muscles rigid. *Touché.*

He indicated the ledger lying open on the desk. "This goes beyond money disappearing from the Holiday Market. Much deeper."

Emma's heart stuttered. "What do you mean?"

"The town's finances have been … creatively managed for generations," Gus explained, his tone grave. "Once, your parents mentioned that they always suspected something was off with Sweetwater Springs' past."

"They were history buffs."

"Yes, but they never found this." He tapped the ledger. The pages were brittle and yellowed with age. "This is a piece of the puzzle."

"None of this explains why you reached out to me," she countered. "If this is about the Holiday Market's finances, Elliot and Victor are handling it. Besides, we shouldn't even be here. There are **NO TRESSPASSING** signs all over the place."

"My family still technically owns the property. The mill has been in the Stratton family for generations. The signs keep out vandals and thrill-seekers. As the owner, I may invite anyone here."

Emma nodded, relieved to have a legitimate explanation. Before she could ask more, a floorboard creaked behind her. She whirled, her flashlight beam landing on a familiar face.

"Olivia?" Emma asked.

Her friend stepped forward. "I followed you," Olivia admitted. "I was worried when I saw you leave your bakery in such a rush."

"I didn't see any car headlights."

"I stayed well behind you."

They huddled around the ledger as Gus explained its importance. The deeper they delved, the more unsettling the story became. Hidden transactions. Secret accounts. Agreements that had shaped the town's growth—and possibly its downfall.

"Who's behind all this?" Emma asked.

Gus opened his mouth, presumably to answer, but before he could speak, the crunch of footsteps outside silenced him. The room plunged into a tense hush.

The door swung open.

Emma heard her own shallow breathing until a male voice called out.

"Emma? Are you in here?"

Victor.

Relief washed over her, tempered with the last remnants of tension from the night. "Yes, I'm here."

Victor stepped inside, his expression a blend of concern and exasperation. "What is going on?" His eyes flicked between Emma, Olivia, and Gus, taking in the scene with growing confusion. "Emma, I saw your note at the bakery. There were no lights in your apartment upstairs, either."

"So, you decided to waltz into my bakery?"

"The unlocked back door concerned me."

"We found something." Emma held up the ledger. "A major development that explains some discrepancies in the town's finances."

Victor crossed the room. "This clarifies a lot," he stated when Gus finished explaining. "However, it also raises more questions. Who has maintained this secret accounting system all these years?"

"The million-dollar question." Emma shook her head. "This affects the whole town."

His hand landed on her shoulder. "First, we get this ledger somewhere safe; cross-reference it with the official records. Then we take our findings to the sheriff."

The intensity in his gaze sent a shiver through Emma—not of fear but an inexplicable emotion. Something unspoken.

"The Holiday Market begins in a few days," Olivia reminded.

"Therefore, we work fast," he replied. "Emma, is it possible for us to use your bakery as a base of operations? It's private, and no one will suspect anything if we go in and out.

Plus, Olivia's bookshop is next door, and she obviously won't report us."

"Yes. I'm happy to assist." Emma nodded. "Take the storage area off the back room. We'll set up chairs and a couple of my café tables. I'll keep the ledger there."

"Perfect," he said. "Gus, make copies of every page. Olivia, you and Daniel pull any relevant town records you can access without raising eyebrows."

As they walked to their cars a few minutes later, Emma broke the silence. "Victor ... I ... thank you for coming tonight."

"I was worried. I mean that." He turned to her, his expression easing. "And I should thank *you*."

"For what?"

A faint smile tugged at the edges of his lips. "For being you. For having the courage to chase this, even when it would be easy to look away."

They held each other's gazes for a moment longer. Then they drove back in separate cars. Victor's headlights reflected in her mirror, a constant presence as he trailed her down the road, a silent guardian ensuring her safe return to town.

THE NEXT MORNING, Emma woke to the pulsing thud of hammers. She drew open the white lace curtains and peered out the window. Across the street, carpenters erected wooden stalls. Mayor Thompson supervised with mittened hands as he directed the placement of some wreaths.

After a shower and a breakfast, she threw her parka over fitted dark jeans and a sweater and ventured outside. The scent of sawdust merged with evergreen, and she nearly collided with Mrs. Chen. A tangle of popcorn and cranberry garlands dwarfed the woman's petite frame.

"Oh, Emma dear! Perfect timing. Can you lend a hand?" Mrs. Chen asked.

Together, they wound the garlands around a stall. Other volunteers strung tiny white lights. Their laughter and chatter flooded the square, starkly different from the previous night's anxious whispers.

As Emma admired their handiwork, Sheriff Randall appeared. His broad shoulders filled out his long wool coat, and his hands rested habitually on his belt.

He stayed apart from the commotion, deep in conversation with a deputy. Their hushed tones and tense postures spoke volumes.

This was indeed serious.

"Thank you for jumping in like this, Emma," Victor said as he approached. The morning light caught the sharp angles of his jawline, softening as it played across his warm hazel eyes.

"You thanked me last night."

"I'm thanking you again. It couldn't be easy, given … everything."

"Because I'm becoming a hermit?"

"Hardly," he replied. "You're in town with me.'"

A thin layer of frost clung to the grass, glinting like scattered diamonds in the pale sunlight. The air carried a sharp, clean scent, hinting at the possibility of snow.

"Well, it feels good to be useful again," she admitted. Gathering her courage, she added, "Victor, regarding the conversation we had about that complication."

"What complication?"

"When you were in Venice, you called and mentioned a complication. I rushed you off the phone because a customer had walked into the bakery, but I always wondered. You never finished explaining."

"I uncovered a cache of shipping manifests from the spice

trade era. Part-time work for me, but I couldn't leave until I solved it."

"Solved what?"

"The pepper, Emma. Black pepper. The quantities never added up, and everyone assumed it was because of poor bookkeeping."

"Black pepper? We're talking about black pepper?"

"Yes. The variations corresponded to a complex code. Once I cracked it, it revealed information about secret cargo —jewels, artifacts, you name it. I wanted to document everything properly."

"So, you didn't forget me here in Sweetwater Springs?"

"On the contrary. If I remember correctly, I asked you to come to Venice in that same conversation, didn't I?"

"I wanted to, and I regretted not taking the chance, not seeing where it might lead. I was afraid. I had a business to consider."

"And now?" An intensity passed between them that had nothing to do with black pepper or Venice. How long had it been since anyone had looked at her like that—like she was the center of someone's universe? The town pulsed around her, the scent of pine and garlands, but there was also a warmth building between them that made her heart beat in a way she hadn't felt in a long time.

Emma fidgeted with the sleeves of her parka. "I still have a business, and I'm still scared."

"You can't live in regret," he said, his voice lowering, drawing her in. "We can start something new right here, right now."

"Maybe you're right," she said.

A crash at the town hall cut through the air. All eyes turned toward the building's dark windows.

For a split-second, everything went still. Then, a figure

darted from a side door that led to the basement, disappearing into the shadows before anyone could react.

"Lock down the area!" Sheriff Randall shouted to his deputies as people scrambled. Emma's throat constricted. The sheriff was never one for dramatics unless it was critical.

Victor's hand on her elbow steadied her. "The ledger," he murmured, his voice barely audible above the commotion. "Where is it?"

"On a shelf in the storage room of my bakery." Emma swallowed hard, her mind spinning with all the implications. The town she'd grown up in, the people she'd known her entire life—everything intertwined, more tangled than she could've ever imagined. She glanced at Victor, feeling his calm presence beside her.

"I'm coming with you," he said. "We shouldn't take any chances. Don't worry. We'll fix this," he murmured, as if reading her thoughts.

CHAPTER 4

*V*ictor guided Emma away from the commotion, the turmoil fading into a distant murmur as they walked toward her bakery. He pictured the familiar CLOSED sign hanging in the window—an unwelcome fixture these days. Her financial troubles hovered at the edges of his thoughts, weighing on him like the first heavy snowfall of the season, quiet but inescapable.

Behind them, Sheriff Randall's voice shouted, "I want this entire building searched, top to bottom."

Sweetwater Springs wore its festive attire with understated elegance. Gossamer strands of fairy lights wove between wrought-iron lampposts, lending an otherworldly sheen. The shop owners had transformed the usually pragmatic and tidy shop windows into enchanting scenes—miniature worlds that beckoned passersby to pause and remember the magic of the season.

The air carried a medley of scents: the sharp pine of fir boughs, the heady spices of mulled cider, and beneath it all, the cool, clean scent of snow.

With his hands deep in his coat pockets, Victor watched

the townsfolk bustle about, their easy camaraderie contrasting starkly with the transient life he'd always known. Sweetwater Springs seemed like a place where people belonged—a concept foreign to him, a man more accustomed to terminals and hotel rooms than hearths and homes.

And then there was Emma. When he observed her behind the counter of her bakery, cinnamon and sugar swirling in the air, a sensation stirred inside him, a pull toward a possibility he'd never allowed himself to consider. Could this town be home?

Back at the bakery, updates on the investigation trickled in throughout the day. Olivia called, sounding frustrated. The sheriff's team had hit a wall when they found a locked safe in the basement, even though the mysterious figure had vanished.

Victor's instincts nagged at him. There was a key clue they were missing, a puzzle piece somehow out of reach.

The usual activity had given way to a hushed reverence, as if Sweetwater Springs itself was appreciating its holiday makeover.

In the bakery's back room, Victor sifted through ledgers, the columns of numbers blurring after hours of searching for patterns, for something—anything—that might unlock the town's secrets. The inviting scent of cinnamon and butter wafted through the bakery, tugging at his concentration.

Through the doorway, he watched Emma, completely immersed in her baking. She moved with practiced grace, pulling tray after tray of snickerdoodles from the oven, cooling them on racks, and carefully wrapping each one. Her precision was soothing, a contrast to the tension that had been building in him since they'd started this investigation.

Now and then, she disappeared into the basement, arms full of cookies destined for the freezer. The sweet aromas called him from his task, drawing him into the heart of the bakery. The steady hum of the mixers, the rhythmic thump of dough being shaped—it all seemed strangely reminiscent of coming home.

He couldn't resist sneaking a cookie or two, earning himself a delicate raised eyebrow and a half-hidden smile from Emma.

"Victor, these are for the Holiday Market," she scolded, her tone halfhearted.

"No one's going to miss a couple," he teased, biting into another.

"How about *ten?*" she shot back, swatting his hand from grabbing another cookie.

He smiled. The heat from the oven had loosened her ponytail beneath her hairnet, leaving wisps of wavy golden hair framing her face. Her eyes, as clear and blue as the sky over Venice, were brighter, more alive. For an instant, she seemed like the Emma he'd known before—carefree, with a laugh that made him want to stay.

As the afternoon wore on, he became more distracted—not by the case, but by her. Watching her move through the cooking area, he decided they both needed a break. Maybe a chance to clear their heads, and ... a chance to confront the unspoken strain that had built between them.

He stood, stretching, then cleared his throat. "We've been at this all day," he began, his voice breaking the comfortable quiet.

She glanced up, wiping her hands on her apron. "Yes, but time flies when you're busy. I'd forgotten how much I enjoy baking. Lately, I haven't been myself."

"That's understandable. We all have times like that."

"Are you getting philosophical on me?" she teased.

"Only practical." He closed the ledgers. "How about dinner? We've survived on cookies long enough, and at this rate, I'll be carrying an extra thirty pounds by Christmas." He patted his stomach.

She laughed, the sound light and sweet. "I sincerely doubt it."

"Yet you bake all day and still look perfect." He grinned, drinking in the sight of her—flour-dusted apron, her complexion smooth and radiant, the rosy flush of someone who spent her days kissed by the warmth of an oven. Or from his compliment. He wasn't sure.

"Occupational hazard, tasting little bites here and there." She paused, "So, dinner?"

"The Sweetwater Inn," he suggested, keeping his tone casual. "Their grilled salmon is perfection. My treat."

Emma hesitated, then nodded. "Why not?"

As they stepped outside, the snowfall had thickened, blanketing the streets in a pristine layer of white. Streetlamps lined the way, the light refracting off each crystal like a thousand tiny stars.

Victor stole a glance at her. Her navy parka cinched at her narrow waist, with the faux fur of her hood framing her face. Her brown leather boots left a neat trail behind them as they walked side by side. His own wool coat, a relic from his years of travel, seemed out of place here. He pulled his cashmere scarf tighter, observing the clear distinction between his sophisticated, wandering lifestyle and the simple, steady rhythm of this town—and this woman.

The silence between them was easy, yet charged with unsaid words.

"Remember the last time you were in Sweetwater Springs?" she asked quietly, breaking the stillness.

His stride faltered, memories rushing back. "How could I forget?"

He recalled each moment vividly. The fresh spring air, heavy with the scent of barbecue and sweet corn. Fireflies dancing in the twilight. The two of them, escaping the crowd, found a tranquil spot beneath an old oak tree. The moonlight had played across her beautiful features.

"We were arguing about … what was it?" she asked.

"The proper method to make s'mores." He chuckled. "You were adamant about using artisanal chocolate."

"I'm an authority on sweets. However, you insisted it wasn't a real s'more unless the chocolate came from a vending machine."

Nostalgia tinged their laughter. For a heartbeat, the time they'd spent apart melted away, leaving only the memory of what might have been.

"I thought you were going to kiss me that night," she said, her tone slightly above a whisper.

He turned to her, snowflakes catching on her golden lashes. Her blue eyes, luminous in the moonlight, held the question he'd asked himself a thousand times since that evening.

"I wanted to," he admitted, his voice rough with truth. "More than anything. Raindrop."

Her breath hitched at the familiar nickname. It wasn't just a word. It was a memory, a bittersweet reminder of what might have been. She met his eyes, the depth of longing there was undeniable. Her question, when it came, was little more than a sigh. "Why didn't you?"

He sighed. A mist lingered in the chill night air, suspended between them. "I was leaving. Inheriting a fortune, moving from place to place, never settling. Meeting you was never part of the plan. I couldn't start something, knowing I'd have to end it."

A flicker of hurt passed across her face. "Why?"

He gathered his thoughts. The streetlight illuminated her upturned face, accentuating the vulnerability in her expression.

"I didn't know how to belong anywhere, Emma. I've spent my whole life traveling. When I came here, I told myself it was temporary." He peered at the snowy road. "Sweetwater Springs wasn't supposed to be part of my story."

"Is it really so hard to imagine staying in one place?" she asked.

"For me, it was," he admitted. "I didn't know how to stop."

"You stayed in touch. At least for a while."

"It was impossible to let go of what we had," he confessed. "Even as I kept moving, I thought about you. I couldn't forget you, but I was afraid of what connection meant, tying me down to one place."

Her gaze never left his face. "And now?"

"And now I'm here, because I couldn't stay away."

The words were fragile, and full of unspoken possibilities. The wind stilled, as if the universe itself waited for what might come next.

A sudden gust broke the spell. They hurried through the streets, the quiet expanding between them once more.

"You're walking better," she noted.

He smiled. "Physical therapy helped. Plus, the Mediterranean diet wasn't bad either."

She shot him a sidelong glance. "You spent time in Venice, right?"

"Yeah," he said. "Gorgeous city, incredible history. I was consulting on a restoration project for some ancient buildings before I started my accounting job there."

"You actually enjoyed working in accounting?"

He grinned. "I did. It reminded me of an FBI seminar I took once. Fascinating stuff."

"FBI?" she repeated. "It's amazing how much about you I don't know."

"There's time to learn," he said softly. "Financial records

tell stories. Even in a town such as Sweetwater Springs, there are patterns if you look closely."

They stopped at a crosswalk, and while they waited for the light to change, she asked, "Do you think someone's hiding something?"

"Definitely a possibility. The discrepancies I found aren't the work of amateurs. Someone has siphoned off money for years, all in the name of preserving town heritage," he replied. "Modest variations spread out over decades, each one insignificant on its own, though adding up to substantial sums. This is a classic technique for hiding financial irregularities in plain sight."

"If they thought they were doing the right thing..." she trailed off.

"Even if the intentions were good," he said, "the end doesn't justify the means."

The walk signal blinked on, and they continued across the street.

Soon, they reached the Sweetwater Inn.

The inn's timeless elegance always attracted Emma. With its exposed beams and crackling hearth, the place exuded a luxury that matched the heartening simplicity of their meal —perfectly seared salmon, roasted root vegetables, and a slice of huckleberry pie they shared between them. She praised the dessert as a rare triumph, graciously conceding to the innkeeper's skill, though she inwardly compared it to her own creations.

After dinner, they wandered down the main street. When they passed the park, Victor reached for her hand, the gesture so natural, it felt as if he'd done it a hundred times before.

"Let's take a walk around the lake," he suggested.

Under the pale December sky, the water gleamed silver,

its surface undisturbed and reflective. Fragile ice crystals formed intricate patterns along the shallower edge.

The scene was so serene that it could've been painted.

"Emma," Victor began. "I heard that life hasn't been easy for you. If you ever want to talk, I'm here."

Her shoulders tensed. "People have been gossiping about me?"

"Not gossip," he reassured. "Concerned friends. Elliot, Nora, Olivia, Daniel, … they mentioned your bakery has been closed for a while."

Emma looked out across the frozen expanse of the lake. "Business has always been good."

"And your reputation is impeccable," he added.

"Thanks. Though that's not the topic, is it?" Her voice faltered. "After my parents passed, I started holding on to items. Their recipes, kitchen gadgets, trinkets—things that don't even matter. It's gotten bad, Victor. My apartment is a disaster. I can't think in there, let alone ask for help." She blew out a breath. "Even the bakery is a mess. You know that. You've seen it."

He stepped closer, taking her hands. "The situation isn't as bleak as it seems."

"I'm trying, I really am, but it's overwhelming."

This wasn't solely about the clutter; it was about everything she'd been carrying, all the grief and fear that had trapped her in a circle of things rather than people.

"Emma," Victor said, his gaze locking with hers. "Just to make it clear, I'm not going anywhere."

She considered telling him everything—her unhappiness, her isolation, the relentless grip of her parents' memory. Instead, she gave a weak smile. "Thank you. For listening."

He grinned, that familiar spark of humor in his eyes. "One of my many talents."

She met his gaze, seeing nothing but acceptance.

After they left the lake, they passed Mr. Garrison's antique shop and the miniature Christmas village in the window. The sight made them both smile.

Before they walked further, they spotted a silver-haired woman struggling under the weight of her groceries. Without hesitation, Victor hurried to help and relieve her of the bags.

"Mrs. Miller," he greeted. "Let me carry these for you."

Her eyes crinkled at the corners. "Victor Steele! You're Elliot's cousin, aren't you?"

He said with a grin, "We are related."

"You and Elliot are almost twins."

"That's what people say." He shot a cheeky smile toward Emma while offering his arm to Mrs. Miller. "Shall we escort you to your doorstep?"

"I live a couple of blocks away."

"No worries. Happy to assist."

As the trio ambled along, an ache bloomed in Emma's ribcage. Victor's kindness, his amiable smile—it was hard to reconcile this man with the one who claimed to be a wanderer.

Observing his tender interactions—the way he clung to Mrs. Miller's every word, his patient pace matching her shuffling steps—ignited a spark. Each shared laugh, each soothing touch on the older woman's elbow, wove an invisible thread, binding Emma's heart more tightly to his. By the time they reached her bakery, the moon hung high in the sky, casting light over the snow-covered town.

"You're really passionate about your work, aren't you?" Emma asked, pausing at her bakery's door.

His expression softened. "Solving a puzzle that has real-world consequences is exactly what I've always wanted to do."

"And the FBI?"

He smiled, a touch of sheepishness in his eyes. "The FBI would provide me with the opportunity on a grander scale. Bigger cases, more impact, and their resources would allow for tackling larger, more complex financial crimes. Plus, the chance to travel doesn't hurt."

"I've never been outside the U.S.," she admitted.

"You should. That's why I invited you to Venice."

"Maybe someday," she said. "I honestly would love to go."

"Venice was amazing, but when Elliot called me, I accepted without a second thought. This community, these residents matter more to me than I realized."

"Would you have returned here if Elliot hadn't called you?"

"Yes." He replied immediately.

She gazed up and down the street at the decorated storefronts. "The town has a way of getting under your skin. So beautiful, isn't it?"

His eyes, however, were on her. "Yes, it is," he agreed. "Emma, again, if you ever want to talk about anything, I'm here."

She drew a quick, uneven breath at the sincerity in his voice. She had kept her struggles to herself for a considerable amount of time, and it felt foreign to even consider sharing them.

"Thank you for a wonderful evening," she whispered.

He leaned in, brushing a kiss against her cheek. "Goodnight, Raindrop."

As he walked away, something within her shifted. For the first time in ages, hope flickered in her chest. Whatever tomorrow might bring, she knew she wouldn't have to deal with it alone.

Summoning a breath of determination, she fished out her keys, unlocking the door and stepping inside the bakery to face the chaos.

Emma trudged up the narrow staircase to her apartment, her stomach tightening as she flicked on the lights. Boxes stacked high with baking supplies and tools poking out like bizarre sentinels from a sea of cardboard greeted her. She sank into the worn armchair, the only empty space available in the room.

Sighing, she glanced around, the realization of how far things had deteriorated sinking in. Her parents' belongings, long untouched, blocked her path to the bedroom. Piles of sentimental knick-knacks buried the kitchen.

Her eyes landed on the shelf where her grandmother's jewelry box sat. The jewelry box, a treasure she had admired but rarely accessed, had a polished cherry wood finish and an intricate inlay of pale flowers. She lifted it and placed it on her bed, outlining its ornate carvings. She had lost the winding key years ago.

Hesitantly, she opened the lid. The expected tinkling melody didn't play, but the gleam of costume jewelry caught the light, each piece telling its own story. She fingered a string of faux pearls that her grandmother had worn to every Christmas Eve service. A gaudy brooch in the shape of a peacock, its tail fanned out in an array of colorful rhinestones, had been a favorite for summer picnics. A delicate cameo on a thin gold chain bore the profile of a woman with remarkably similar features to Emma—a family heirloom passed down through generations.

Among the jewelry, she found handwritten notes, each a window into her grandmother's life. One, written on pale blue stationery, detailed the story of a pair of clip-on earrings—a gift from a secret admirer at a USO dance in 1943. Another note, its edges worn soft with handling, contained a recipe for snickerdoodles, complete with tips for stretching rations during wartime.

Nestled in the corner, barely visible, was a folded piece of paper and a sketch of a lighthouse.

Sweetwater Springs once boasted a magnificent lighthouse, but it had long since vanished, replaced by the town hall. What did the lighthouse on the paper symbolize?

She shimmied sideways through the narrow path to her bathroom, requiring the balance of a tightrope walker. Her bed was a compact island in a vast ocean of possessions, calling out to her.

Though sleep, like so many things, had become a luxury.

Her gaze snagged on a stack of her mother's recipes on the bureau. One more sorting, she promised herself. One more, and maybe she'd find the elusive peace that brought everything back together.

Hours slipped by as Emma lost herself in the ritual of touching, remembering, and categorizing. Each item was a tether to a time when her little orbit made sense, when laughter resonated through the bakery and the future was bright and limitless.

The first tentative rays of dawn crept in, finding her curled in her armchair.

Another day. Another battle to carve out room to simply exist and fight against the rising tide of her possessions.

She was baking again, certainly a good sign. Also, she contemplated opening her bakery to the public, because her minimal savings only lasted so long. Plus, her entrepreneurial spirit reminded her that this was the holiday season and delivered the highest earnings of the year.

Beneath her trepidation, a flicker of optimism expanded. The mystery of the ledger, the tendrils of connection, and Victor—they murmured of a world beyond these walls. A world that, despite her fears, still had a place for her.

She stood, stretching muscles taut from another night of

restlessness. Tomorrow, she would clear one corner of her apartment. Just one. A defiant act against the clutter that threatened to swallow her whole.

And for the first time in months, that felt like enough.

CHAPTER 5

The rhythm of Emma and Victor's following days settled into a familiar cadence, the quiet persistence of the investigation intertwining with the demands of the holidays. *Blissful Bites*, once a silent testament to Emma's struggles, hummed with renewed purpose as she prepared for the Holiday Market.

On a morning a week later, she plunked herself in the middle of her bakery, wrapped in a cocoon of contentment and spice. The fragrant aroma of vanilla melded with the sharp tang of nutmeg. Her hands moved with practiced grace, arranging golden butter cookies on a polished silver tray, each one a triumph of flavor and artistry.

In the back storage room, Victor's presence was a constant reassurance. The rustle of papers and the occasional tap of his pen counterbalanced the recurring whir of mixers and the clink of baking sheets.

Emma reviewed her handiwork with a mixture of pride and trepidation. Each perfectly formed cookie represented more than a contribution to the Holiday Market; it reclaimed her life and her passion.

She'd shared some of her findings with Victor—the jewelry box and the lighthouse. Though he'd looked into it, nothing concrete had emerged.

A loud knock broke through the bakery's calm. Emma glanced toward the back and met Victor's gaze. His brow furrowed, silently questioning who was knocking so early. The CLOSED sign hung on the door.

Through the glass, Lillian Weatherly's face appeared, her silver hair impeccably styled even at this hour.

Emma sighed, wiping her hands on her apron before heading to the entrance. "Lillian," she greeted, trying to mask her surprise as she opened the door. "I'm not open yet. How's Theodore?"

Lillian breezed in without missing a beat. "Oh, my handsome StormyCuddle is busy composing his latest masterpiece. A verse about snowflakes and stardust."

Emma smiled. The nickname, a combination of Theodore's surname, Weatherly, and Lillian's affectionate moniker, "Cuddle," never failed to amuse. Despite their years apart, the bond between Lillian and Theodore was indisputable.

"Sweetheart, I'm here with a purpose," Lillian said. Though pale from a recent illness, her eyes were sharp as they scanned the bakery, lingering on the partially open storage room door. "Is that Victor Steele I see back there? Quite the striking figure you've got helping you."

Emma swallowed hard, willing the prickling heat to subside as it inched upward on her cheeks. "He's assisting with some paperwork," she replied, deflecting. "What can I do for you?"

"The children's choir could use a treat after their rehearsal today," Lillian declared, her tone leaving no room for negotiation. "Of course, you were the first person to come to mind."

Emma hesitated, her eyes darting to the half-finished trays of cookies. "I'm not sure I have the time—"

"Nonsense," Lillian waved away her protests. "The choir is rehearsing for the Luminary Walk. And, between us," she tilted her head, her voice dropping to a hushed tone, "a bit of holiday magic from *Blissful Bites* is exactly what this town needs."

Emma's resistance wavered. "Alright," she conceded, "I'll make a quick batch and send it with you."

Lillian smiled, triumphant. "You're coming, too."

Emma opened her mouth to refuse, but Lillian's arched brow silenced her.

Emma knew better than to argue. Lillian had a will of iron, honed by decades of stubborn determination and an unwavering belief in her own rightness.

"Alright," Emma agreed with a sigh, "if you insist."

"That's the spirit," Lillian said brightly. "I'll pop into Olivia's bookstore next door and come back for you in an hour."

Once she was gone, Emma surveyed her kitchen, ingredients laid out for the cookies she'd promised. This wasn't only about the choir. It was a reminder that *Blissful Bites*, and by extension, she herself, still held a place in the heart of Sweetwater Springs.

She reached for her mother's recipe box, fingers grazing the familiar edges. "Alright, Mom," she whispered, "let's do this."

The mixer whirred to life, and butter and sugar creamed together.

This was more than baking. It was a connection to her parents, to her past. The bittersweet ache of their absence was there, but today it was more like a gentle nudge than a gaping wound.

"*Blissful Bites* will endure," she vowed. "I'll make sure of it."

After setting the cookies to cool, Emma slipped upstairs to her apartment to change. She opened her closet and paused. The disorderly shelves closed in on her, and her hand froze midway. When was the last time she'd actually seen the full contents of her wardrobe?

The idea of sorting through even this small area was daunting. However, maybe these were the moments to create more room—within her closet, her home, and her life.

Maybe.

The notion clung to her, as persistent as the scent of cinnamon that always seemed to follow her from the bakery.

A few minutes later, she stepped back downstairs.

She'd taken care with her appearance, wearing a cashmere turtleneck in a deep burgundy that complemented her golden hair. Dark wash jeans hugged her curves, tucked into supple leather boots that had seen her through many a Sweetwater Springs winter. A cream-colored wool coat, cinched at the waist, completed her ensemble.

"All set," she called toward the back storage room.

Victor's pen paused at her voice. He stood and appeared in the doorway, his intense eyes taking in her appearance with quiet appreciation.

"You look beautiful, Raindrop," he said softly. "That cream-colored coat suits you."

Her heart fluttered, and she ducked her head, feeling suddenly shy. "It's just something I threw on."

He smiled, stepping closer. "You have excellent taste." His deep voice sent a shiver down her spine that had nothing to do with the winter chill. "Be careful out there."

She got lost in the intensity of his eyes, but Lillian's call from outside jolted her back to reality. With a quick grin, Emma headed for the door.

"Promise you won't work too hard while I'm gone and stay away from my cookies," she said.

Victor's chuckle followed her. "No promises."

She grinned and hurried out to a waiting Lillian, and the two women set off for the community center. The scent of fir trees tinged the cold air, and Sweetwater Springs, with all its charm and quirks, had never felt more like home.

Along the way, Lillian regaled Emma with the latest town chatter. Emma attempted to listen, but her mind was split. Her thoughts kept drifting back to Victor—the enigma he presented and the gladness that he'd brought into her life.

Lillian went on to tell Emma that Mr. McAllister had nearly set fire to his home toasting bread, and his son, young James, was supposed to craft a spectacular ice sculpture for the market's centerpiece.

Emma raised a brow, sensing the doubt in Lillian's tone. "What do you mean, he's supposed to?"

Lillian waved a dismissive hand. "Oh, you know James. He's charming enough, but people only put up with him because of his parents. He's always trying, but forever falling short."

"James isn't a child anymore," Emma pointed out. "He's a grown man."

"Grown or not," Lillian shrugged, "some habits are hard to break. Friends and family still treat him like he's that aimless boy. It's easier than admitting he hasn't quite found his way."

Emma glanced at her. "How's his business going?"

"*McAllister's Game Haven?*" Lillian shook her head. "It had its moment. A novelty at first, but the excitement fizzled out. People drifted away."

Their pace quickened as fat snowflakes fell, heavy and wet, melting the instant they touched Emma's skin. The Pacific Northwest continuously found itself caught between two worlds, never fully embracing the sharp bite of winter or the steady drizzle of rain.

As they rounded the corner, the tempting sweetness of caramelized sugar wafted from a café, and she inhaled appreciatively.

Five minutes later, Lillian insisted on ducking into a yarn shop, leaving Emma to wait outside. She had no intention of listening in on the quiet conversation between Mayor Thompson and Sheriff Randall nearby, but snippets of their exchange floated to her ears.

"Jim, we need to address those discrepancies—" the sheriff's voice was low, serious.

"Not here," the mayor interrupted, his usually genial tone sharpening. He was a stocky man with glossy silver hair and ruddy cheeks. As if on cue, his face transformed into a beaming smile when he spotted Emma. "Ah, Emma! You look radiant today. Is that something sweet I see in the box?"

Emma returned his smile. "Christmas cookies for the choir kids, mayor. They're rehearsing today."

A rare moment of sincerity broke through his features. "Your parents would be proud of you."

Emma offered a polite smile, though her mind churned with questions.

What discrepancies?

Soon after Lillian came out of the yarn shop, the women entered the community center.

Lillian opted to sit and watch from the sidelines. The lively commotion of children dressed as angels and shepherds brightened the atmosphere, tinsel trailing behind them like crooked halos.

Delilah Fitzwater, ever the vibrant spectacle, was at the center of the commotion. Her latest hairstyle was a cascade of purple streaks, while a glittering star-shaped clip adorned her bright red blouse. She noticed Emma and hurried over.

"Thank goodness you're here." Delilah threw her arms

around Emma in an exuberant hug. "We need those cookies —desperately."

Emma surveyed the room, chaos reigning as children in angel wings darted between chairs and laughter bounced off the walls. "Are you positive? Looks like they've already had plenty of sugar and sweets."

"Oh, trust me, they're more than ready." Delilah grinned. "I'm counting on these cookies to give them that last burst of energy before sending them home to their parents."

Emma raised an eyebrow as she hung her coat. "That's your brilliant plan? Sugar them up and then send them off?"

"Exactly!" Delilah laughed, unabashed. "Mothers and fathers get an extremely active child for a few hours; we get peace and quiet. A flawless strategy."

Shaking her head, Emma set the box of butter cookies on the table. "That's a strategy to make everyone's day interesting."

"Here's to making their day—and ours—a little sweeter." Delilah snatched up a cookie, devouring it in one quick bite before wiping the crumbs off her blouse. "Now that you're here, think you could lend a hand with these costumes?"

Emma studied the crumpled tunic Delilah held up, clearly unfinished with its uneven hem and fraying edges. The coarse fabric hung awkwardly, shapeless, as if begging for some order. "I came here to deliver cookies, not join a sewing circle."

"Too bad, sugar plum. You're in it now." Delilah winked, handing her a needle and thread. "Time to play seamstress."

After the children and their parents left, Emma joined the other women. Before long, she was knee-deep in sequins, tulle, and frayed fabric. She smoothed out jagged seams, adjusted hemlines, and, with a few swift tweaks, transformed the haphazard into something heavenly.

Just as Emma tied off the last stitch, the door swung open,

and Sheriff Randall stepped inside. He tilted back his broad-brimmed hat, its dark-brown surface beaded with moisture. His expression was tense, his gaze scanning the room with a practiced air of authority. The cheerful clamor quieted to a murmur.

"Folks," he said, his voice low but carrying an unmistakable seriousness. "Someone tampered with that safe in the basement—the one everyone's been wondering about."

A collective gasp rippled through the gathering.

Victor had appeared at Emma's side, his solid presence grounding her.

"What does this mean for the Holiday Market?" Delilah's voice sliced through the murmurs.

Sheriff Randall shifted, but Mayor Thompson came forward, his face set in a smooth mask. "Nothing's being canceled," he assured, his tone louder than necessary. He clapped his hands with forced enthusiasm. "Now, who's with me?"

A scattered cheer rose in response, yet the unease beneath the surface was palpable.

Theodore Weatherly entered the center, his gaze sweeping over the crowd until it landed on Lillian. She visibly perked up at the sight of him, her hands smoothing her hair, though they trembled slightly. Beside Theodore, Mr. McAllister—always eager to be part of the action—nodded vigorously to a conversation only he seemed to have. His Santa hat sat askew, nearly falling off after hours of entertaining children, but he made no move to adjust it, apparently too caught up in his own musings.

"We will need volunteers, though," Sheriff Randall continued. "To guard the town hall. We'll keep it covered around the clock. Any takers?"

Hands shot up instantly, as if the entire room had been holding their breath for the chance to help. Even with the unsettling news, the resilient spirit of Sweetwater Springs came forward. Conversations droned to impromptu fundraising efforts and offers to dip into personal savings. The town's heart beat strong, unwavering in its resolve to protect what mattered most.

While Emma was wiping crumbs from the table, she overheard snippets of more serious discussions questioning, "What will happen to the school programs if we don't resolve this embezzlement soon?"

A cold realization gripped her. The community, its cherished way of life, was on the line. Losing their autonomy, fracturing the close-knit bonds that held them together, sent a shiver through her. This investigation wasn't solely about catching a culprit; it was about preserving everything that made this town her home.

Victor lightly touched her elbow. "Emma, a word?"

"Of course."

He steered her toward a quieter corner, his tone dropping as he asked, "Have you given any more thought to the lighthouse?"

Surprised by the sudden shift, she tilted her head. "Why?"

"You placed the note and jewelry box on the counter in the back room," he replied.

She blinked. "I did?" She tried to recall, although the turmoil of recent days had blurred her memory. She'd left them there in a rush, distracted by everything else on her mind. "I thought I put them away …"

"Hercule Poirot would find it disappointing," Victor chuckled, though his eyes remained serious. "You need to keep better track of your evidence."

"There's no connection between the lighthouse and the current investigation. You said so yourself."

He shrugged. "Things can change. Fast."

Before she could press him further, the door to the

community center swung open again, this time with a bang, and Gus Stratton hurried in. His face was flushed, and his breath came in short, excited bursts as though he'd run straight from the historical society.

"I've found something!" Gus's voice rang out, and every eye turned toward him. His gaze flitted between Emma and Victor before locking onto Delilah, who stood, arms crossed, curious but skeptical.

"What?" Delilah asked.

"I discovered a document tucked away in an acid-free box in the archive room. It mentions a lighthouse—and a connection to the town hall site."

Internally, Emma's thoughts spun in a flurry of alarm and disbelief as the lighthouse, the mystery she had been quietly puzzling over, suddenly thrust itself into the open, unraveling like a carefully guarded secret in front of everyone.

How much did Gus know? What exactly had he uncovered? And, most crucially, how would this revelation affect the investigation?

Outwardly, she fought to maintain a composed facade, gripping the edge of a chair as she forced a calm breath. When she finally spoke, she measured her voice, betraying none of the turmoil roiling beneath the surface.

"A lighthouse, you say?" Her gaze flicked toward Victor, who raised an eyebrow in silent acknowledgment. "What kind of connection are you referring to, Gus?"

Gus, oblivious to their unspoken exchange, turned his attention to Delilah, a broad grin splitting his face. "Well, hello there, gorgeous! Did you do something new with your hair, or is that just the glow from my cataracts?"

Delilah rolled her eyes, despite the corners of her mouth twitching. "Oh, Gus. Your eyesight may be failing, but your charm? Unyielding as ever. I just can't tell if that's a compliment or a concern."

"Always a compliment," he replied, stepping over to plant a kiss on her cheek.

They'd rekindled their high school relationship, and even though they hadn't set a wedding date, their love was clear.

"Looks like their sparks are rekindling rapidly," Emma whispered to Victor.

He raised an eyebrow. "Small town romance at its finest."

She grinned. "Let's hope they don't take another fifty years to figure it out."

Gus slipped an arm around Delilah's shoulders, his entire demeanor softening. "Sorry to interrupt your sewing. I figured you'd all want to hear this right away."

Delilah patted his hand, her numerous bangles jingling merrily. "I love a good mystery, my sweet potato. I may even write a song about it."

"I'm all ears. Your tunes are, how shall I put this— unique?" Gus's voice dropped to a murmur, eliciting a round of uncomfortable chuckles from those closest to him. Delilah, once the town's go-to matchmaker, had shifted her focus to music in recent years, although her enthusiasm far outstripped her talent. Still, no one could deny the happiness she brought with her ukulele and spontaneous songs, even if they occasionally made for a challenging listen.

Emma cleared her throat and cut through the affectionate banter. "Delilah, before you compose, perhaps we should concentrate on the mystery at hand. Victor and I were discussing some related matters."

Victor gave a slight nod, picking up on her cue. "Yes, we came across information that might overlap with what you've found, Gus. Can you share more about that document?"

The room was still buzzing with chatter, and Gus hesitated, his gaze flicking around at the others. "Why don't we step over there?" He lowered his voice. "This isn't a conversation anyone should overhear."

With a nod of agreement, the small group followed him, and Gus grinned as they approached the refreshment table. "And look—chairs for us by the cookie trays. Two birds, one stone, eh?"

Once they settled in a tight circle, away from prying ears, Gus began.

"The document I found belonged to none other than Abigail Sweetwater herself. It describes the lighthouse as a 'beacon of secrets' and refers to a hidden chamber beneath the old town hall site." He paused, obviously savoring the suspense he was building. "Here's the kicker—the entry dates back to 1872. A full decade before we have any official record of a lighthouse even being built in Sweetwater Springs."

"That's quite the discovery, Gus," Emma said slowly. "Especially considering what I came across."

"Don't keep us in suspense, sugar plum!" Delilah chimed in. "Spill!"

Emma breathed in deeply. "I recently came across my grandmother's jewelry box."

"Didn't you have it all along?" Delilah asked.

"Yes, although I never really inspected it. Inside, on a piece of paper, was a sketch of a lighthouse."

"You've been keeping this from us?" Gus inquired.

"I didn't see how it related to our investigation and assumed it wasn't relevant," Emma said defensively. "Victor agreed."

Victor stepped in. "We don't have all the pieces yet. There was no clear connection until now."

Gus ran a hand through his thinning hair. "This lighthouse mystery might be crucial to everything we've been looking for." He leaned back, his excitement tempered by the gravity of the situation. "The past has a funny way of staying hidden until the right moment, doesn't it?"

Emma exchanged a glance with Victor, a flicker of unease passing between them. The lighthouse had suddenly become the center of something far larger—and more dangerous— than they could have imagined.

"Bring your finding to the historical society," Gus urged. "Some pages in the document are water-damaged, but I made out a reference to a 'key to the town's future' hidden within the lighthouse's walls."

"A lighthouse that isn't there anymore," Victor pointed out.

After a brief discussion, Emma and Victor exited the community center. The early darkness of the Pacific Northwest winter had settled in, wrapping the world in misty twilight. A fine drizzle turned Christmas lights on various houses into red and green halos. The scent of damp fir needles blended with woodsmoke from distant chimneys, creating an atmosphere both melancholy and comfortable.

As they stepped further, a plaintive mew echoed through the chilly silence.

Emma halted, her gaze drifting over the snow-dusted shrubbery. "Did you hear that?"

"Sounds like a cat," Victor replied, gesturing toward a cluster of bushes near the building's entrance. "Probably from over there."

Emma crouched down. "Hello? Is anyone there?" she called, peering through the branches.

A tiny, shivering kitten peeked out, its fur fluffed up against the cold. Bright blue eyes peered at her from a bedraggled face. The white kitten, only a few weeks old, shivered pitifully.

It let out another soft mew, as if pleading for help.

"Oh, you're so sweet," Emma cooed, carefully scooping up

the frigid bundle. The kitten nuzzled into her, purring faintly.

Victor knelt beside her, a smile softening his features. "Looks like we have an unexpected visitor."

"We can't leave it here."

Victor clucked sympathetically. "Nora might consider accepting it. She and Elliot were discussing pet ownership. First, let's warm this little one up."

As they returned to the community center, Emma cradled the kitten close against her chest.

Soon, the kitten became an instant celebrity. The volunteers offered names and snacks. Even Delilah gushed over it.

"Finding a stray kitten during the holidays brings good luck," she declared. "This little one is the magic Sweetwater Springs needs."

Emma stroked the soft fur. Perhaps Delilah was right. In the middle of the riddles and confusion, the kitten brought joy and laughter.

As the evening wore on, Emma frequently checked on it, curled up in a makeshift bed of fabric scraps.

Before the center closed for the evening, Delilah had adopted the kitten, promising to inform Elliot and Nora.

Soon afterward, Emma and Victor meandered along Main Street, their figures cutting dark silhouettes against the muted glow of storefronts. The bare cherry blossom trees loomed overhead, their branches etched against the sky. Night had draped itself over the town, hushing the day's commotion.

Emma nestled closer to Victor. "What's next?" she asked.

His arm encircled her waist. "We'll continue our investigation and consult the Holiday Market committee. They might've detected something we overlooked. In addition, we'll delve deeper into the lighthouse mystery."

As they approached *Blissful Bites*, Emma spotted Olivia hanging wreaths on her bookshop's front window.

"Emma, Victor!" Olivia called, turning to face them. "I was hoping to catch you both. Daniel and I are continuing to review the donation files, and there are definitely discrepancies."

"Any idea who is behind it?" Emma asked.

"Welcome to the challenging and costly search," Olivia replied, as she finished placing the last wreath with a sigh. "Only a select few have access to those records, and they're all trusted members of the community. Let's head inside your bakery, shall we?"

Once in the back storage room, Olivia retrieved a stack of papers filled with columns of numbers.

"The discrepancies were subtle at first," she explained, spreading the papers out before them. "Although they've become more brazen over time."

"Have you traced any of the current missing funds?" Victor asked.

With a measured pause, Olivia countered, "That's the tricky part. The money seems to vanish. There are no unusual local deposits or irregular purchases. Who in Sweetwater Springs could orchestrate such an elaborate scheme?"

Before the discussion could continue, a brisk tapping on the door interrupted them. Gus Stratton poked his head inside. "I figured you'd all be here. Sorry to disturb, but there's something else." He stepped in, unfolding a weathered map of Sweetwater Springs. "I went through more files in the society's basement. This is from the 1950s and reveals a fascinating detail."

They huddled around, following Gus's finger trace a discolored line. "See this? Here's a tunnel system, running directly under Main Street. Most of it has probably caved in by now, but—"

"But if any of it is still accessible," Victor finished, "it might explain how the money is disappearing without a trace."

The idea of hidden underground passages stirred a thrill of excitement and apprehension in Emma. What other secrets could they conceal?

Olivia and Gus departed soon afterward, leaving the air charged with unspoken revelations and prolonged tension.

In two swift strides, Victor closed the distance between them. Emma sank into his embrace, feeling the solid strength of his chest. His hands cradled her face, his thumbs caressing her cheeks, drawing her closer as he lowered his lips to hers.

The kiss was a delicate dance of tenderness and passion, a promise whispered in the moment's hush—an unspoken vow of shared desires. When they parted, he rested his forehead against hers, the intimacy of the gesture sending a thrill through her.

"I have to go," he murmured, his voice thick with emotion.

Her fingers curled into the fabric of his collar, anchoring herself to him. "I know," she whispered.

He pulled back, his eyes searching hers with a depth of emotion that made her heart pound. "Promise me you'll lock up tight and sleep. There are more mysteries to unravel, and I need you sharp."

"I promise," she replied.

With a final, prolonged kiss, Victor stepped away, the reassurance of his presence still pervasive. He turned slightly, a playful smile curving his lips. "Sweet dreams, Raindrop," he said, his voice rich with affection, a secret shared only between them.

As the door clicked shut behind him, she touched her lips where the intensity of his kiss lingered, faint and sweet. Despite the fatigue settling into her bones, her mind hummed with anticipation, both for the investigation that lay ahead and for the deepening connection she felt with Victor.

Her gaze drifted to a shelf crammed with baking tins and inherited cookie cutters, nostalgia washing over her. Her hand hovered over a dented star-shaped cutter and memories flooded back—Christmas mornings spent happily baking with her mother, laughter and flour dancing in the air. The Holiday Market committee had suggested she use more modern, festive shapes for her cookies this year, but that simple star spoke of home and heritage.

Her fingers closed tightly around the cutter, its familiar edges pressing into her palm, as if it, too, held onto her as much as she held onto it. The thought of setting it aside and breaking the tradition her mother had started so many years ago saddened her. What if altering things meant losing more than a piece of the past? What if modernizing the bakery, like everyone suggested, left behind the core of what *Blissful Bites* truly was?

The thought of letting go felt like losing her parents all over again.

She placed the cutter on the shelf, her hand trembling. She couldn't bring herself to toss it into the donation box. "One more year," she murmured, though a pang of guilt echoed in the back of her mind. She had made the same promise to herself last Christmas. And the Christmas before that.

As she stood there, a quiet realization dawned. Maybe revitalizing the bakery, like Victor had revitalized her heart, didn't mean erasing the past. Maybe it meant honoring it in a manner that enabled her to move forward. Could there be a way to do both?

She exhaled slowly, her fingers brushing the edges of the cutter once more before pulling away. Tomorrow would bring more answers—about the lighthouse, about her grandmother's secrets, and about the possibilities she hadn't yet imagined.

For tonight, she allowed herself to believe that sometimes holding onto the past and stepping into the future didn't have to be mutually exclusive. Perhaps, just perhaps, she would find the courage to do both.

The thought brought a smile as she turned off the lights and locked the door behind her.

CHAPTER 6

*T*wo days later, Emma awoke to the insistent buzzing of her cellphone vibrating on her nightstand. Groaning, she fumbled in the dark, blinking as the screen's brightness pierced the morning gloom.

She scanned a text from Victor:

Meet me at the lumber camp. 7 AM. Bring coffee. And some of your cookies.

A tired smile tugged at her lips, even though it was far too early for grinning. She turned and squinted at the clock. 6:15 AM. Barely enough time to shower, get dressed, and brew a pot of coffee. Yet, as she moved through the quiet motions of her morning routine, her mind churned with curiosity. Why the lumber camp? And why at this hour?

She opted for practicality, sliding on a pair of well-worn jeans and a chunky-knit sweater in a blanket plaid. She layered a thermal shirt underneath for extra insulation against the morning chill. Her favorite brown leather boots, their soles thick enough to navigate icy sidewalks, completed the outfit. Finally, she wrapped a hand-knitted scarf—a gift from her grandmother—around her neck, its familiar weight comforting against the uncertainty of the day ahead.

The scent of freshly ground coffee filled her small kitchen, mingling with the aroma of her signature snicker-doodle cookies, which had been cooling on the counter from the previous evening's baking. She carefully packed a few into a tin, poured the coffee in a thermos, and packed napkins and two mugs.

Her thoughts drifted to Victor. The memory of their last kiss remained—potent, and undeniably distracting.

By the time she slipped on her coat and stepped outside, dawn cast a muted light over Sweetwater Springs. The sky was a pale palette, streaked with hints of pink and muted grays. The streetlamps faded, and the air was sharp in her lungs, promising a clear winter day.

She drove to the mill and noticed that the streets were eerily deserted. She neared the outskirts of town, the mill's familiar silhouette ahead, stark against the rising sun.

Victor was already there, leaning against his car, hands stuffed in his jacket pockets as she pulled up. His tall frame stood outlined against the morning light. She approached, balancing a thermos and cookie tin, noting the tension in his stance.

"Good morning," she greeted, handing him the thermos with a mischievous smile. "Here's your bribe."

He accepted with a grateful nod. "You know me too well."

"And the cookies?" She handed him the tin. "These better be worth the early wake-up call."

He chuckled, but the sound was brief, his attention already shifting toward the mill. "There's something you need to see."

They scooted under the chain link fence with the **NO TRESSPASSING** sign and entered the building. "Weren't we researching lighthouses?"

He didn't answer, motioning for her to follow as he led the way toward a side entrance. The door creaked loudly, revealing the mill's shadowy interior. Sunlight filtered through cracked windows, forming faint patterns on the dust-covered floorboards.

He stopped near a stack of crates. "Gus mentioned the tunnels under the town, but I believe there's more to it."

Emma frowned, glancing around the empty mill. "You think the tunnels extend this far?"

"Not likely," he replied, "but anything's possible."

She trailed him to the same office as their meeting with Gus. She set the thermos on a table, then poured two steaming mugs of black coffee, their shared preference.

"Ah, thank you." He smiled. "Exactly what I needed."

She placed several cookies on a napkin and handed them to him. "Not the most nutritious food to eat in the morning," she noted.

"Cookies are breakfast muffins that haven't gone to finishing school yet." He examined the cookies with exaggerated seriousness. "Practically a health food."

"Ah yes." She nodded with mock seriousness. "All the rage in fitness circles, I'm sure."

He took a bite of one cookie, then set it down, his fingers drumming a thoughtful beat on the table. "This place has been abandoned for years, but what if it's not a historical relic? What if someone's using it as a hideout?"

"Merely a hunch," he continued, at her questioning glance. "Although worth checking out. Don't forget the name of those crazy streets—"

They finished their coffee and cookies and proceeded through the mill, avoiding the cobweb-draped machinery.

Victor pointed to a faint series of footprints in the dust. "Someone's been here recently."

The trail led them deeper into the mill's interior. They stopped at a back office, its door hanging precariously by a single hinge, a relic of what had once been solid oak. The stench of mold and decay saturated the air, thick and suffocating.

Inside were remnants of ruined furniture, collapsed shelves, and forgotten pieces of a past long neglected. A stack of papers rested on a desk.

Emma's gaze flickered across the papers. "Another ledger," she murmured. "The dates, the amounts—they match the missing funds."

Victor scanned the pages, and his usual composure faltered. "We've got them," he said, his voice low but resolute. Then, as if remembering something crucial, he added, "However, there's also a different matter."

With deliberate care, he moved aside a stack of boxes in the corner, revealing what had been hidden beneath layers of grime and debris: a trapdoor, nearly indistinguishable from the rotting floorboards.

Emma's breath hitched, a shiver of unease snaking through her. "What is that?"

His fingers brushed the edges of the door. "I'm not sure yet, but it might be the key to understanding how everything's connected—the missing funds, the lighthouse, the secrets buried beneath Sweetwater Springs." When he looked at her, something deeper flickered in his eyes—concern, perhaps, or the burden of the unknown. "Will you go down there with me?"

Her heart beat double time. She wasn't one to shy away from a mystery, but there was a certain quality about the way he spoke, the gravity in his tone, that made this discovery more significant than anything they'd uncovered before.

"I will." She crouched beside him, her fingers trailing over the wooden door. It felt cool beneath her touch, ancient and forgotten. "But are you sure about this?"

"I wouldn't ask if I wasn't."

Her pulse quickened, not only from the anticipation of what they might find but from the awareness of Victor beside her—the solid warmth of his hand, the power in his quiet authority.

"Okay. Let's do it," she said.

He gave her a brief nod before pulling a small flashlight from his pocket. He flipped it on, casting a thin beam of light over the trapdoor. With a grunt, he lifted the heavy panel, revealing a set of stone steps that descended into darkness.

Emma peered into the depths. Her instincts warred between caution and curiosity, but the urge to uncover the truth, to stand beside Victor no matter what they faced, was stronger than her fear.

"After you," he said, his tone light, his gaze sober.

She shot him a look and couldn't suppress a smile. "You really know how to sweep a girl off her feet."

He chuckled, his eyes brightening by a fraction. "I'll make it up to you."

Before Emma could reply, a noise came from the hallway —a faint scuffling, growing louder with each step.

"We need to move," Victor whispered, his tone sharp and urgent.

Without hesitation, Emma shadowed him down the stairway. The temperature dropped, the chill settling in her bones as the musty scent of damp earth surrounded them. At the bottom, Victor's flashlight threw a narrow beam of light across the space. Shelves lined the walls, their surfaces sagging under the mass of dust-covered documents.

"What is this place?" Emma breathed, her voice barely audible in the stillness.

"We may have stumbled upon Sweetwater Springs' secret archives," he replied.

Words formed on her lips, but before she could speak, the footsteps above grew louder, more insistent. Victor clicked off the flashlight, plunging them into blackness.

She tensed, her pulse quickening as the intimacy of their closeness became impossible to ignore. The brief contact of his arm against hers sparked a heightened awareness, intensified by the danger surrounding them.

The footsteps halted at the top of the stairs, and a voice, deep and familiar, shouted, "Hello? Is anyone down there?"

Emma's eyes widened. Sheriff Randall.

Victor remained still, his body rigid beside hers. She shifted subtly, her lips grazing his ear as she whispered, "We should say something."

He nodded. "Here, Sheriff," he called. "It's Victor Steele and Emma Jacobsen."

A beam of light sliced through the gloom, illuminating their faces as the sheriff descended the stairs. His presence, solid and authoritative, dominated the small space.

"Mind explaining why the two of you are trespassing in a condemned building at dawn?" Sheriff Randall asked, his tone more curious than accusatory. He glanced around, eyes narrowing as he took in the rotting structure. "This place is dangerous—unstable floorboards, crumbling walls. It's not safe."

"Gus Stratton told us his family owns this property," Victor replied calmly. "He gave us permission to be here."

The sheriff's gaze canvassed the room. "I don't see Gus anywhere."

"He isn't with us today, but he was here the other day," Victor said. "Why did you decide to come here this morning?"

"I saw cars parked in front."

"But why here? Why now?" Victor asked.

"The mayor told me he heard reports of people snooping around the old camp. He wanted me to take a look in the morning."

"We're not trying to cause trouble," Victor replied. "I believe this place is being used as a hideout. It might be tied to the missing donations."

Sheriff Randall arched an eyebrow. "And you failed to bring this to my attention first?"

Emma, sensing the sheriff's growing frustration, stepped forward. "We didn't want to jump to conclusions. We were trying to confirm our suspicions before bothering you."

The sheriff exhaled heavily. "Well, you've got my attention. Show me what you've found."

Victor led the way back up the stairs, the air growing warmer as they left the damp room behind. He directed the sheriff to the office they had explored earlier; the room filled with the stale scent of forgotten paperwork and neglect. Emma advanced toward the ledgers stacked on the desk, brushing off the dirt that hung on their surfaces. Opening an aged volume, she revealed columns of handwritten numbers and names, all dating from decades ago.

Sheriff Randall peered over her shoulder, his expression hardening as he took in the contents. "This is something." He pointed to a particularly incriminating entry. "If these records are accurate, it establishes an obvious trail of theft."

Victor nodded. "That's what I was thinking. Someone's been hiding out here, possibly this morning. We just missed them."

The sheriff's eyes narrowed further. "You're sure it wasn't only the two of you?"

Victor's gaze met his. "I'm certain. There were fresh signs when we arrived."

Sheriff Randall considered this, then nodded grimly. "I'll

get a team out here; sweep the place. If there's any more evidence, we'll find it. But next time," his voice dropped with unmistakable authority, "you come to me first. Understood?"

"Absolutely," Emma replied.

In the stuffy office, as Sweetwater Springs' buried truths emerged, a prickle of tension ran through her, warning that the real threat hadn't shown up yet.

CHAPTER 7

*W*eak sunlight filtered through a heavy blanket of clouds, creating a muted beam over Sweetwater Springs as the town slowly stirred to life. Emma entered her bakery before dawn, the air laced with the remnants of a cold night. She moved quietly, her thoughts churning.

In the back storage room, the ledger sat on the table, holding secrets that potentially unraveled everything—or worse, revealed more than they bargained for. Emma stared at it, her mind grappling with the town's financial crisis, the cracks widening beneath the surface. She had hoped that uncovering the truth might be a step toward fixing Sweetwater Springs, but the reality of her own struggles was hard to ignore.

Yesterday's earnings had been pitiful, hardly enough to cover the bakery's endless overhead expenses. No matter how many cookies and cakes she sold, the numbers didn't add up. Bills were piling up—rent, utilities, supplies. She glanced at the stack of unpaid invoices in the corner of her desk, an imminent reminder of how close she was to losing everything she'd worked so hard to build. The irony gnawed at her—here she was, trying to save Sweetwater Springs from financial ruin, while her own business was on the brink of collapse.

Emma sank into a chair, her hand resting on her mother's favorite cookbook. Her heart clenched as she considered her parents—how they'd poured their love into this place, making *Blissful Bites* a cornerstone of the community. Could she truly let that legacy slip through her fingers? How was it possible to continue the investigation and unravel the town's mysteries when her own world was unraveling right along with it?

She couldn't sit here indefinitely, lost in worry. The kitchen called to her, and if there was anything that grounded her, it was baking.

She stood, rolling her shoulders back as if shedding the burden, and walked to the counter. Flour dusted her hands as she reached for the mixing bowl, her mind shifting with the rhythm of preparation. She grabbed ingredients without thinking, muscle memory guiding her.

The steady thump of kneading dough under her palms became therapy, her thoughts gradually softening with every fold and press. She prepared a batch of scones, ripe with cranberries and orange zest.

An hour later, the kitchen pulsed with the fragrant aroma of gingerbread and toasted almonds, a delicious herald of holiday cheer rising from the oven.

Victor stepped into the bakery, his silhouette framed against the early morning light, carrying a paper bag in one hand and two steaming cups of coffee in the other. His eyes found Emma, busy at the counter, molasses smudging her apron.

"Thought you might need reinforcements," he said, lifting the coffee in an offering.

She glanced over her shoulder, wiping her hands on a dish towel. "I could've brewed some."

He raised a brow, his smile tender. "You, my Raindrop, have plenty on your plate already."

The corners of her mouth lifted in delight. "My hero."

As she wiped the counter, Victor shrugged off his coat and stepped to a café table. Instead of sitting, Emma mixed batter for another batch of gingerbread, her hands working effortlessly. He set the coffee down, then reached into a bag marked with the Sweetwater Springs Inn logo, pulling out a container of fruit salad.

"You came prepared," she remarked, pouring the batter into baking pans.

"I figured we should eat something healthy before diving into all this." He motioned toward the newest ledger, sitting like an unwelcome guest on the table in the back, then opened the fruit container. The tangy aroma of apples and sun-ripened berries provided a refreshing counterpoint to the bakery's spice-laden air.

"Good call." Emma wiped her hands on her apron and moved to the back room. Returning to the café, she set the ledger she'd retrieved on the table.

She paused, her gaze on Victor as he set out their makeshift breakfast. Today, his usual sleek style was replaced with a more rugged charm. His Henley shirt hugged his broad shoulders, the fabric a soft heather gray that brought out the ruggedness of his frame. The rolled up sleeves revealed the lean strength of his forearms. His dark hair, often meticulously styled, fell in tousled waves, softening the sharp lines of his face.

A small nick on his chin hinted at a rushed shave, giving

him a roguish, endearing look that made her smile to herself. There was something undeniably magnetic about this unpolished version of him.

"You're a lifesaver," she said, grabbing a slice of apple as she sat at the table. "I've been so wrapped up in baking, I completely forgot about breakfast."

He flashed a grin, one side lifting just enough to crease the corners of his eyes. "Can't let Sweetwater Springs' finest baker run on empty, can we?" He slid into the chair across from her, his fingers idly circling the rim of his coffee cup. "So," he murmured, his tone shifting, "where do we begin?"

"I went through this ledger again." She pointed to a series of entries from the 1950s. "There's something off about these numbers. And look—each one has this strange symbol beside it."

Victor leaned in. "It's a code."

The bell above the shop door chimed, breaking through the moment. Emma's hand paused mid-reach for her coffee, her heart skipping as her gaze flicked to the entrance.

Dr. George Carter, the town's veterinarian, strode in. His usually relaxed, genial expression had hardened, and his steps carried an urgency that hadn't been there before.

"Emma, I hope you're open," he said as he stepped inside. His gaze shifted, taking in Victor's presence. "Am I interrupting anything?"

"Not at all, George." Emma shot him a quick smile. "I planned on opening soon and had unlocked the door. How's the kitten doing?"

"The kitten's fine, and Delilah Fitzwater has officially adopted her. Named her Snowflake. I'm guessing you already heard?"

"We did," Victor and Emma replied in sync.

"That's not why I'm here, though." George's chin dipped, a

stiff, mechanical movement, and his gaze zeroed in on the ledger lying open on the table. "I see you've found it."

Victor's brows knitted together. "Found what, exactly?"

"May I sit?" George gestured toward a chair as Emma nodded. He draped his coat over a chair and settled into a seat, his demeanor shifting to quiet reflection. "The ledger belonged to my great uncle. He served as the town vet back in the 1950s."

"I wasn't aware," Emma replied. She moved to the kitchen, arranging several warm scones, plates, and napkins on a tray. When she returned, she offered a scone to George. "Please help yourself. They just came out of the oven. I can brew some coffee, too."

"No need." His smile widened, eyes creasing at the corners. At thirty-five, George had quickly become a beloved figure in Sweetwater Springs, his kind disposition drawing more than a few admiring glances. His sturdy frame hinted at days spent wrangling livestock and nights hunched over operating tables.

"Thank you for this, though." As he reached for a scone, the sleeve of his fitted navy sweater pulled back, revealing an intricate compass tattoo etched on his inner wrist. A sheepish grin crossed his face. "A reminder of my wilder college days," he said.

Emma wondered about the story behind that tattoo—the adventures that had led him to this point. Was the compass a symbol of a pivotal moment in his life, or perhaps a guiding principle he still followed?

"So, your great uncle was a vet," she said, drawing their conversation back to the topic at hand.

"I haven't shared that information with many people," George admitted. "No real reason to."

"How does this tie into what we're dealing with now?" she pressed.

George let out a long sigh. "He did more than record animal treatments. His ledgers contained details about the town's secrets—things those certain influential individuals wanted to keep under wraps."

"As in?" Victor asked.

"Mostly financial irregularities," George replied, breaking off a corner of his scone. "He also noted connections to some less-than-legal operations. I came across his notes while setting up my practice, and I've been trying to piece it all together since."

Emma wrapped her hands around her warm coffee cup. "Do you think any of this could be linked to the current situation?"

"I do," George replied. "His records revealed a pattern of unusual financial transactions extending to the 1950s. Large sums of money flowed through Sweetwater Springs, and none of it ever appeared in official paperwork."

Emma's fingers tightened around her cup. "Exactly like the current situation."

"Yes," George affirmed, leaning back in his chair. "I've heard all about the suspected embezzlement. The ledger indicates frequent visits from out-of-town 'businessmen' to a lighthouse."

Victor paused midsip. "The old lighthouse? That's been gone for years."

"Right," George replied. "However, my great uncle's notes hint that there might have been hidden spaces inside, possibly even underground passages. When they constructed the town hall, those passages could have been sealed off or integrated into the foundation of the new building."

"The tunnels Gus mentioned!" Emma said.

George tilted his head. "Tunnels? What tunnels?"

She hastily filled him in on Gus's discovery of the map, revealing tunnel systems under Main Street.

George nodded slowly. "That fits. My great uncle's notes mention 'unseen pathways,' but I never understood what he meant. If these exist and connect to the town hall, they explain how money has been moving around undetected, both then and now."

"Why are you telling us this?" Victor asked.

George sighed. "Because history is repeating itself. The patterns in the current financial discrepancies match those from the 50s almost exactly. Someone has revived the old system, and I'm concerned about what else they might be reviving. The town hall's renovation last year possibly uncovered these old passages, allowing a person or persons the opportunity to exploit them again."

After George left, a contemplative silence settled over the bakery.

Victor's attention was irresistibly drawn to Emma. The way her finger traced the rim of her cup held him captive, a gesture so familiar yet tinged with an intimacy he couldn't define. Her delicate eyebrows were furrowed, her thoughts clearly distant.

Everything beyond them faded away, leaving only the two of them. He yearned to reach across the table, to still her hand and unlock the secrets behind that pensive expression. The air between them felt charged, though neither spoke a word.

He redirected his focus. "George was certainly informative," he remarked.

Emma met his gaze, her eyes sparkling with curiosity and determination. "This adds a whole new dimension to what we've discovered, doesn't it?"

"Let's not lose sight of where we started." He set aside the fruit and scones and dragged the ledger closer, flipping back to the page they'd examined before George's arrival. "You were saying something about odd entries from the 1950s?"

"Right, yes." Her shoulder touched his as she displayed a series of numbers. "See these? A strange symbol comes after each one."

He studied the enigmatic symbols, acutely aware of Emma's closeness. Her scent, a blend of vanilla and cinnamon, enveloped him, threatening to derail his concentration. He inhaled deeply, steadying himself.

"These markings aren't arbitrary," he stated. "There is a discernible pattern at play here."

He shifted his gaze back to her, momentarily taken aback by the fire in her eyes. The deep blue gleamed with fierce determination, mirroring her resolute spirit. A wayward strand of hair danced across her cheek, and his fingers twitched with the urge to tuck it behind her ear, battling against the need to maintain his composure.

This was not the moment for intimacy; professionalism had to take precedence.

"You're not going to drop any of this, are you?" he asked.

Her smile was a tantalizing mix of defiance and charm. "You know me well enough. Once I catch a whiff of a mystery ..."

"You chase it to the bitter end," he completed, a hint of admiration in his voice.

Inwardly, he shook his head; aware he was in danger of being captivated by more than the enigma at hand. Emma's fierce determination and unwavering quest for the truth were magnetic.

These were qualities he respected—the tenacity to seek honesty, regardless of where it might lead.

"Any other thoughts?" he asked.

As Emma pondered, the intensity of her focus, the slight way her lips turned as she concentrated, stirred something profound within him.

No matter what secrets were concealed within the ledger,

an undeniable truth resonated in his heart: there wasn't a single other person he'd want to navigate this journey with; nobody made untangling life's complexities as thrilling as Emma. In that instant, the mystery faded into the background.

All that mattered was her.

CHAPTER 8

The following afternoon, Emma stepped into the community center, her arms laden with boxes of butter cookies. She dressed warmly for the moody December skies in a knitted sweater, and dark jeans, topped with a wool coat. A snug red scarf wrapped around her neck added a splash of color, while a well-worn leather satchel hung from her shoulder, its strap crossing her chest.

Inside the center, an eruption of commotion met her, bursting forth like confetti. Handmade paper chains zigzagged across the ceiling, interspersed with strings of mismatched lights that blinked in exuberant disarray. In the center stood a lopsided pine tree, its branches sagging under the bulk of eclectic ornaments—clearly the enthusiastic handiwork of eager little hands.

The air teemed with the spicy scent of gingerbread and the unmistakable tang of peppermint. A chorus of off-key carols was accompanied by the rhythmic thumping of what sounded like a one-man-band of pots and pans.

As she navigated the colorful chaos, her heart warmed at the sight of friends and neighbors decorating, laughing, and sharing the season's spirit. Children darted around, red-faced with excitement and exertion.

A group of girls huddled near the tree, pointing and giggling at the decorations, while a pair of boys, still wearing their choir robes, chased each other with tinsel garlands trailing behind them like shimmering kite tails.

She smiled. This was the essence of Sweetwater Springs, the heartbeat of neighborhoods—a bond that flourished even in the chill of winter.

She spotted Delilah, and the sweet feline perched regally on her shoulder. Snowflake's white fur contrasted with Delilah's ruby red sweater, one paw playfully swatting at Delilah's dangling silver bell earrings.

"Emma, sugar plum!" Delilah's voice rose above the din. "You won't believe what my little rascal did last night."

Emma dodged a toy reindeer that went sailing past her. She set the cookies on a table decorated with a cheery snowman-patterned cloth.

"Oh?" she asked when she reached Delilah. "What did Snowflake do now?"

Delilah took a deep breath, as though she struggled to contain the story itching to spill out. "I was sorting through boxes in the attic with Elliot, and Snowflake kept pawing at this ancient-looking document. When I unrolled it, can you imagine what I discovered?"

Victor strode in, his tall frame enveloped in a charcoal wool coat. A red and gray plaid scarf peeked out from beneath his collar, and his hands were tucked in leather gloves. The wind had tousled his usually neat hair.

"Let me take a wild guess," he said, stepping up behind Emma and plucking a couple of butter cookies from one box. "Another clue about the lighthouse?"

"Exactly! Gus and I have discussed it at length." Delilah nodded vigorously. "I found a map, dated 1872. And right there, clear as day, is a marking for a lighthouse, though here's the kicker. It's not where we thought it was."

"It stood where the town hall currently is located," Victor said.

"Nope." Delilah shook her head. "Try again."

"Can we examine it?" Emma asked.

As Delilah fetched the map, Emma sensed the heat of Victor's presence close beside her. The fresh scent of earth and pine clung to him, a reminder of the wild beauty surrounding Sweetwater Springs. Momentarily captivated, she felt that familiar heart flutter when she gazed at him.

She shook off the distraction and redirected her focus.

The brittle map was a revelation. Discolored lines tracked the recognizable contours of the town, with notable differences. The map showed only the forest. There, at the edge of the park, a lighthouse overlooked the lake.

"Wow," Victor murmured, his breath tickling Emma's ear. "This is unexpected."

She blinked, and the noisy community center melted away. In a heartbeat, she found herself transported to old Sweetwater Springs—a town finding its feet, full of hope and promise.

A tug on her sleeve snapped her to the present. Delilah was asking something, but Emma couldn't answer because the doors swung open.

Sheriff Randall stepped inside, his easygoing air replaced with a stiffness that set Emma on edge. He scanned the room, briefly resting on the kids before landing on Emma, Victor, and Delilah.

His smile didn't quite reach his eyes. "Can I have a word outside?" He glanced at the children, still caught up in their activities.

Emma, Victor, and Delilah followed him. Once they were away from curious ears, he gave a quick look over his shoulder, then lowered his tone. "There was a break-in at the town hall last night."

A shiver crept up Emma's spine. Her thoughts tumbled over each other like leaves in a storm. "The volunteers—they're supposed to be keeping watch."

"They were," the sheriff replied, his voice weary. "But people have lives. They can't be there all the time."

"Whoever did this," Delilah's voice dropped to a shocked whisper, "is getting bolder."

Victor's hand slid into Emma's, a discreet way of saying, *I'm here*.

"We should check out the park," he said. "And the lake."

As they prepared to head out with Delilah's map, Snowflake jumped off Delilah's shoulder and made a beeline for the door. The kitten paused, glancing back at them with an expression that almost seemed expectant.

Delilah grinned. "We've got a new partner for this investigation."

Emma scooped up the purring bundle and tucked Snowflake into her satchel, leaving it half-open so the kitten could poke her head out.

"Prepared for an adventure, Snowflake?" She glanced at the kitten and then at Delilah. "Mind if we take her along?"

"Of course. Better not lose her," Delilah teased. "I'm completely attached."

"I won't," Emma promised. With Victor beside her and a surprisingly sharp little kitten, she was ready to uncover whatever secrets remained in Sweetwater Springs.

Even with Victor's slight limp, they weaved through the lively streets, dodging shoppers and clusters of carolers practicing. Voices and energy pulsed through the town—the tinny jingle of a charity bell, the crunch of salt underfoot, and the distant melody of *White Christmas* coming from the square.

Twilight would soon creep in, the dwindling daylight splattering the storefronts in shades of amber and indigo. Shop windows glimmered like jewel boxes, their displays throwing playful shapes across the sidewalk. Together, they performed a whimsical shadow puppet show, where reflections sparkled and swirled, creating a dazzling display of light and movement.

The path to the lake wound through snow-covered pines, their branches sagging. Emma stole glances at Victor, taking in his well-defined jaw, the intensity in his eyes while he studied the map.

"You no longer smoke," she noted.

"No, I don't. Didn't want my clothes and hair smelling like it." He glanced at her. "What brought that up?"

"I've been meaning to ask for a while, but constantly forgot." She wrapped her scarf tighter, grateful for its warmth, a comfort against the biting wind that whipped off the water.

He kept pace beside her, his company a comforting shield.

They rounded the last bend, and the lake came into view. The weak winter sunlight formed a silvery light on the frost-covered branches. A lone jogger, his breath visible in the crisp air, circled the lake, the steel-gray water reflecting an overcast sky.

Snowflake, nestled in Emma's satchel, shifted slightly.

"According to the map, the lighthouse should be right about …" Victor voice trailed off as he scanned the shoreline.

Emma followed his gaze. Shrouded in mist and tangled in overgrown vines, the crumbling stone foundation of a lighthouse emerged from the landscape. Its rough outline was nearly lost to time, although the circular shape hinted at what had once stood there.

"I can't believe I never noticed this." Her fingers trembled as she reached into her coat pocket, pulling out the photograph she'd found in the bakery. "This photo—it shows a lighthouse right here, by the lake."

"Funny how the most obvious things can stay hidden in plain sight," Victor said softly. "Though the structure's been gone for years."

Snowflake squirmed and let out a high-pitched meow. Emma set the kitten down, and in an instant, it darted toward the stone foundation, disappearing into the undergrowth.

"Snowflake!" Emma rushed after her, pushing through the brambles, with Victor close behind, his hand steady on her back.

Snowflake sat primly, smug as could be, looking quite pleased with herself.

Victor knelt, clearing away leaves and snow. "Something's carved here. Faded, but it's a date. 18-something?"

Emma squinted at the faint etchings. Before she could react, a shiny object snagged her attention—a glint of metal among the rocks. Carefully, she plucked out a tarnished penny, its copper surface dulled by time but still winking in the weak winter light.

Victor stood and snapped a few pictures. "We'll need to come back with proper tools. More might be hidden here."

Emma crouched for a better look. "Check this out." She pointed to a flat piece of metal wedged between two rocks. "Is this a plaque?"

Victor cleared away more dirt and tangled roots. A brass plate came into view, green with age.

"Nice catch, Emma," he said. "There's an inscription here, but scarcely legible. I can make out 'water's' and 'protect'."

"Could that say 'beacon'?"

The plaque didn't offer any explicit answers, although it

suggested something of importance, possibly even a connection to the lighthouse.

"We should head home," Emma said, standing. "Delilah's probably wondering what happened to her kitten." She carefully placed a now-sleepy Snowflake into her satchel. They prepared to leave, and she took one last look at the foundation.

As they retraced their path, the first stars peeked out, the sky deepening to a velvety indigo. The lights of the town beckoned, reminding her of a realm beyond their discovery, a beacon guiding her home—to a future as bright and full of promise as the constellations.

Victor turned to her, his dark eyes reflecting the starlight. "We did it," he said, reaching for her hand.

A rush of emotion swept through her—relief, exhilaration, and a profound sensation. An emotion that had quietly flourished between them since that initial day that they'd met so many months ago.

"We did," she agreed.

They paused in perfect stillness, the ancient foundation of the lighthouse behind them, the sprawling town stretching out before them. Overhead, the night sky unfolded as if it were a promise—limitless and full of possibilities.

Victor's lips brushed hers, and the kiss carried the sweetness of butter cookies and the thrill of unspoken vows. Emma melted into him, her worries and fears dissolving like sugar, vanishing in the heat of a freshly brewed cup of hot cocoa. The world around them blurred, leaving only the two of them and the spark they shared.

When they finally pulled apart, breathless, Snowflake's impatient meow resonated from her satchel.

Emma laughed softly. "Someone's eager to go home."

"Home," Victor repeated, his voice low, vivid with

newfound meaning. "I'm starting to think Sweetwater Springs could be the place for me."

"Your upbringing was—"

"Cultured, and never settled," he replied. "My family spent more time sailing the Adriatic than putting down roots. I've never really belonged anywhere ... although I'd like to."

You belong here, she thought. *you belong with me.* But she kept the words inside.

Their hands remained clasped as they walked, Snowflake's contented purr blending with the tranquil murmur of the evening. A deep sense of rightness completed her. Regardless of the challenges that lay ahead—regardless of the secrets Sweetwater Springs held—they would face them side by side.

As they neared her bakery, Emma slowed. In the dimly lit window of Mr. Garrison's antique shop, nestled among old-fashioned ornaments, stood a delicate glass lighthouse. Its fragile beacon shimmered faintly, casting an ethereal light.

A chill of anticipation prickled down her spine. The resemblance to the lighthouse sketch she'd found in her grandmother's jewelry box was uncanny. Coincidence? Or something more? The lighthouse's sudden appearance, so soon after their find, felt like more than a fluke—or a sign ...

Perhaps a warning.

She hesitated, biting her lip, debating whether to share her contemplations with Victor. Until she could piece together what it all meant, she kept the thoughts to herself.

Apparently sensing her distraction, Victor looked at her. "You okay?"

Emma forced a brilliant smile. "I'm admiring the decorations," she replied, her voice light, even as her deliberations churned with uncertainty.

CHAPTER 9

*L*ess than two weeks before Christmas, and the Holiday Market crackled with excitement as Emma and Victor jostled through the crowded square. The air was brittle with the promise of more snow and sweetened by the scent of candied almonds and clove-studded oranges. Snowflake, curled in the crook of Emma's arm, purred contentedly, her white fur speckled with silver tinsel from Delilah's enthusiastic decorating.

"Ready for this?" Victor asked, his fingers grazing Emma's shoulder.

She nodded, and he could feel the tension radiating through her body. The documents in his briefcase—from her grandmother's jewelry box, including the lighthouse sketch —grew heavier with each step.

"As ready as I'll ever be," Emma replied. "I'm not sure this is the ideal moment to bring it up, though. It's the first day of the Holiday Market, and everyone's been looking forward to this for weeks."

"There's no perfect time," Victor said. "Might as well be now."

They neared the gazebo where Mayor Thompson stood, ready to kick off the festivities.

"Emma, Victor," the mayor greeted them with a smile. "Here for the opening ceremony?"

"Actually," Victor lowered his voice, "we need to talk to you. Privately."

The mayor's eyes flickered between them and the expectant crowd. His smile faltered. "Can't it wait? We're about to begin—"

"It can't," Emma said. She handed the kitten to a waiting Delilah.

With a resigned sigh, the mayor gestured to an empty tent. Once inside, Victor pulled out his cellphone and scrolled through the photos he'd taken. "These are from the old lighthouse site by the lake," he explained, holding the screen up.

"What lake?" the mayor asked, frowning.

"The one in the park," Victor replied. "The lighthouse was once there."

The mayor shook his head. "You're mistaken. The lighthouse wasn't by the lake. It used to be where the town hall sits now."

"That's what everyone believed," Victor said, "but it's not the truth."

As Emma and Victor explained their discovery, the mayor's expression darkened with a mix of surprise and unease. "An old-timer once mentioned something like this," he muttered, rubbing his chin. "I never imagined it would resurface. What's it got to do with the missing funds?"

"We're not entirely sure," Victor replied. "The real question is, how do we connect the dots?"

A sudden gasp from the crowd outside froze them in place.

Was it a gust of wind sending decorations flying?

They burst out of the tent, only to be met with a shocking scene. Sheriff Randall guided a handcuffed suspect through the crowd, the stunned townspeople parting in silence as they watched.

"George?" Victor blurted out, recognizing the man immediately.

Dr. George Carter's expression was a mask of desperation, his jaw clenched tight, and a vein throbbed at his temple. His wide, frantic eyes darted from one face to another as he fought against the sheriff's firm grip. "I was trying to protect this town!" he yelled, his voice cracking with the strain. Sweat glistened on his forehead, despite the chill. "You don't understand! If the truth comes out, it'll destroy Sweetwater Springs!"

Whispers ripped through the crowd. Neighbors traded worried glances, hugging their children. The festive atmosphere evaporated like mist in the sun.

Emma's icy fingers sought Victor's. He clasped her hand, his thumb tracing slow, calming circles on her skin. She leaned into him, finding solace in his quiet strength.

The mayor stepped forward; his once-jovial face was drawn with concern. He surveyed the square, his shoulders squared beneath a heavy wool coat. Clearing his throat, he raised his arm, and the gathering fell silent.

"I believe," he said, his deep voice carrying, "it's time for a town meeting."

"Now?" someone called out.

"Now," he replied.

Festive sleigh bells jingled faintly in the distance, their cheery sound jarringly out of place in the unsettled atmosphere.

What followed was a meeting like none that Sweetwater Springs had ever experienced. When the truth was disclosed —the correct location of the lighthouse and the trail of missing funds— the tone of the room shifted between outrage and disbelief.

Victor stood at the heart of it, explaining findings with a distinct authority that grew as the day wore on. His quiet determination turned into something sharper, more purposeful. Emma remained beside him, offering him silent strength with each passing glance.

Once the meeting ended, the bustling square emptied, leaving only Emma, Victor, Delilah, and a core assembly of the town's leaders—to face what lay ahead.

"We'll need to dig deeper into the records," Victor said, already piecing together the next steps in his mind. "There's more to uncover."

Sheriff Randall nodded. "I intend to run a full investigation. George wasn't doing this alone."

"Why?" Emma asked, stepping up to the group. "Who else was involved?"

"We're not sure yet, but we intend to find out," the sheriff replied.

"What about the Holiday Market?" Delilah piped up, ever practical. Snowflake sat snugly in her coat pocket. "And the Luminary Walk? The whole town's been preparing for weeks."

The mayor offered a weak smile. "The festivities will go on."

As the improvised meeting adjourned, Victor and Emma stood alone in the square.

Sheriff Randall motioned them aside. "If we don't get ahead of this soon, the state's going to step in. They're already asking questions about how we've been managing things. If they take over ..."

Victor's hands curled into slow fists. "We can't let that happen. We'll find out if anyone else is responsible, no matter what it takes."

"Can they dissolve the council?" Emma asked. "Merge us with Millbrook, although that town is a few miles away?"

The sheriff's nod was gradual. "Probably. And that would be only the beginning. We'd lose everything that makes Sweetwater Springs home." He blew out a sigh as he strode away.

Emma met Victor's gaze, their unspoken resolve solidifying between them.

"You were incredible today," he said, brushing a stray lock of Emma's hair from her cheek.

"You were the one who was amazing," she replied. "Though there are still so many questions, so much left unanswered."

"The truth about the lighthouse is out now," Victor reminded. "That's a big step."

He glanced across the square, taking in the sight of Sweetwater Springs with fresh eyes. The holiday decorations radiated a renewed brilliance, standing bold against the gray sky. Despite the impending uncertainty, the town seemed to shout with a defiant joy, its charm more vivid than ever.

Garlands of recently cut pine draped gracefully from the lampposts, their bright red bows catching the streetlights like flickers of ruby. Glimmering strands of lights wove around the shop windows, each bulb a beacon of hope in the gathering twilight.

The majestic Christmas tree at the center of the square stood tall and proud, its ornaments glinting with renewed brilliance. Tinsel scattered the fading sunlight in dazzling patterns across the ground.

In a storefront, a gingerbread house display beckoned with sugary detail, its tiny candy windows and frosted roof creating a magical miniature world that transported him, for a moment, from reality into the wonder of the season. Everything seemed heightened—the cold, the colors, the scents of pine and cinnamon swirling through the air. Sweetwater Springs, in all its festive glory, was determined to shine brighter in the face of adversity.

"What happens next?" Emma's voice broke through the stillness, her eyes searching his. She could've been asking about the investigation, the town's future, or the unspoken question hanging between them.

Victor turned her until she faced him fully. "We move forward. Together, if you'll have me."

Her smile was soft, but brimming with certainty. "I'd like that."

She rose on her toes, meeting him in a kiss that was unhurried and tender, a noiseless moment of calm amidst the storm. When they finally separated, the noisiness of the day disappeared, leaving them in a tranquil square where everything felt right.

A burst of laughter pulled Emma and Victor's gazes across the square. Delilah commanded a lively group of volunteers, tinsel cascading around her shoulders like a glittering boa. Snowflake perched proudly on the ground, playfully batting at the tiny flurries falling from the sky.

"Shall we?" Victor asked Emma, nodding toward the volunteers, their hands busy with strings of holly and vibrant gold satin ribbons.

Emma linked her arm through his. "Let's spread more holiday cheer, shall we?"

They crossed the intersection, and the first notes of a caroling ensemble reached their ears, a charming backdrop to the festivities. The group was a delightful mix of ages, from bright-eyed children bundled in oversized scarves to elderly couples wrapped in classic woolen mittens. Each scarf—plaid, striped, or solid—brought a whimsical touch to the scene, celebrating the spirit of the season.

Victor's heart swelled as he recognized the familiar

melody of *I'll Be Home for Christmas*. The song rang within him, resonating the truth of belonging he had long sought. Sweetwater Springs had a lengthy road ahead, but this moment held significance, a step toward healing.

His perspective shifted like the kaleidoscope of lights. The holidays were no longer mere rituals from a distant past; they were vibrant bridges to the future, linking memories and hopes alike.

His family's nomadic lifestyle had left little room for cherished Yuletide traditions. Yet here, in Sweetwater Springs, he experienced a whirlwind of community cheer that encompassed countless acts of kindness and shared experiences.

This town wasn't only a place; it was a living, breathing entity of interconnected lives, pulsing with a vitality that both thrilled and terrified him.

When twilight deepened, the holiday lights diminished the encroaching shadows. Each carefully hung ornament whispered stories of resilience and renewal.

He gazed at Emma. Their hands interlaced as if puzzle pieces were finding their match. Whatever squalls lay ahead, they'd weather them, not only as individuals, but as part of this dynamic, imperfect, and special community.

THE WEEK of the Holiday Market unfolded like a vibrant pop-up book, each day unveiling delightful surprises that pulled Emma into its colorful narrative. Though the town reeled from the revelations, its determination to make this Christmas unforgettable shone through.

When the market ended, a sense of melancholy overwhelmed her, but she was cheered because Christmas Day was fast approaching. The season always brought a time for reflection and gratitude. Each year, she attended the morning service, where flickering candlelight and resonant hymns created a sacred, peaceful atmosphere. The nativity scene, lovingly arranged by the townsfolk, served as a poignant reminder of the true essence of the holiday: celebrating the birth of Christ.

In quiet reverence, she contemplated the blessings of the past year and the promises of the new one. For Emma, the season was a blend of heartfelt traditions, communal cheer, and spiritual fulfillment.

Never forget that, she whispered to herself. *Never forget.*

On a Monday morning, a week before Christmas, Emma opened her bakery to find Victor waiting at the front door. His dark eyes gleamed with the kind of mischief that invariably quickened her pulse.

"I have a surprise for you," he murmured, his voice thick with intrigue.

"I'm about to open for the morning rush," she protested, glancing at the clock.

"Not today." He flipped the sign on the door to CLOSED. "Your customers will return, I promise you."

A hesitant laugh escaped her. "What are you up to now, Victor Steele?"

Without a word, he guided her to his car, their intertwined hands in a silent rebellion against the biting dawn air.

They drove out of town, the road winding through a tunnel of pines, resembling watchmen in a scene untouched by time. The purr of the engine blended with the frost-muted landscape, stirring a noiseless hurricane of anticipation beneath her skin.

After what seemed like an eternity, they reached a secluded clearing near the maple woods. The sky, a soft wash of silver, brought a touch of magic to the scene, and Emma's heart thudded expectantly in her chest.

"Close your eyes," he instructed.

Without hesitation, she complied, her muscles coiling with unspent energy as the car door swung open.

The brisk December nipped at her cheeks.

"Okay," he said, his voice laced with intimacy. "Open them."

Emma gasped as she took in the scene. A towering pine stood in the clearing, its roots firmly gripping the forest floor. Compact branches created a natural canopy that embraced the area. At the base of the tree sat an intimate winter picnic, a red and black buffalo plaid blanket spread across a patch of cleared ground, its edges weighted with smooth river stones to keep it anchored against the wind.

Two shiny stainless-steel thermoses stood upright, wisps of steam escaping from their partially opened lids. One released the rich aroma of hot cocoa, while the other promised the spicy flavor of mulled cider.

Beside them, a wicker basket overflowed with a vibrant array of winter fruits. Bright clementines peeked out, their orange skins a cheerful contrast to the snow. Deep purple figs nestled against pale green pears, while a cluster of ruby-red pomegranate sparkled in a glass jar like edible gems.

Two folding camp chairs awaited, draped with snug wool blankets. A string of battery-powered fairy lights flickered from low-hanging branches, washing the enchanted scene in a gentle shimmer.

"Victor, this is so … romantic. How did you …?"

He waggled his dark eyebrows. "I enlisted some help. Turns out, Elliot is quite the outdoor expert."

As if on cue, Elliot emerged from the trees, his wife, Nora, at his side. They waved before disappearing back into the woods, granting Emma and Victor privacy to savor the magical moment.

"Where are they going?" Emma asked.

"I imagine back to town." Victor produced a box of ornaments, each a work of art, hand-painted glass baubles with elusive snowflake designs, tinsel stars, and vintage-style wooden figurines depicting angels and reindeer. "I thought we could decorate our own tree. Away from all the chaos."

Emma's eyes welled up with tears at his thoughtful gesture. "It's wonderful," she whispered.

They spent the morning hanging ornaments, their laughter rippling through the clearing. Victor hung the larger, eye-catching decorations while Emma meticulously positioned the tinier, more intricate ones, adjusting each until it lay seamlessly in the branches like hidden treasures.

Victor hoisted her up, and Emma stretched to set the star on top. She glanced down, taking in their little wonderland. The tree twinkled, the forest hugged close, and Victor's eyes shone with love. Right then, Emma experienced it—a serenity and untamed happiness she'd never known before.

CHAPTER 10

*O*n the Saturday before Christmas, preparations for the children's choir performance and Luminary Walk were in full swing. Emma focused on last-minute costume alterations, her nimble baker's hands mastering intricate stitching. Meanwhile, Victor tackled the prop design, determined to create a backdrop worthy of the town's celebration.

The rehearsal spiraled into mayhem, with one particularly unruly child causing enough havoc to warrant a long time-out. Amid the cacophony, the lighthouse set piece—symbolic of the recent discoveries—swayed ominously. Suddenly, with a bone-jarring crash, it tipped over, splintering wood as it plummeted to the floor, narrowly missing several children who scattered like startled birds.

In the stunned silence, Victor sprang into action. He rushed forward, checking on the kids and cracking jokes to ease their fear. With calm efficiency, he assessed the damage, his keen eye quickly mapping out how to reconstruct the fallen set.

He glanced at Emma, mischief dancing in his dark eyes.

"There goes our beacon of hope," he said with a grin. "Think we could rebuild it using your butter cookies? They're sturdy enough to hold anything together."

Emma laughed, her heart lightening. "My cookies melt in your mouth. Besides, if we used them here, what would you snack on during rehearsals?"

"Fair point," he replied, feigning seriousness. "Can't have me starving, can we? Maybe we need a foundation as solid as my appetite."

"Or perhaps," she teased, "we should keep you away from the set pieces. Your sweet tooth might bring the whole stage down again."

They shared a lighthearted chuckle. Nearby, children giggled, swapping knowing glances at Victor's notorious love for Emma's cookies.

Emma surveyed the shattered lighthouse. "Fortunately, no one was under it."

"Yeah, but it gave us quite a scare," Victor said.

His affable demeanor dissolved the tension, and she admired him as he orchestrated efforts to rebuild, his straightforward leadership radiating confidence.

As the days dwindled down to Christmas, another mystery unfolded. Strange gifts appeared around town—an exquisitely restored antique lamp on the steps of the library, a collection of rare initial prints near Olivia's bookshop, and an anonymous donation for the long-neglected carousel in the park. Each gift came with a note penned in elegant script: "The first rung toward setting things right."

Speculation ran rampant. The recent arrest of Dr. George Carter had been a misunderstanding, quickly rectified once the facts surfaced. He'd attempted to access town records late at night, raising suspicion among locals. He was trying to protect documents he'd inherited from his great uncle, which hinted at the hidden history and financial discrepancies from decades past. Misinterpreting their implications, George believed he was safeguarding the community from a modern-day scandal.

The truth about the gifts came to light when Olivia spotted George's new receptionist, Bailey, sneaking around town. Although he hadn't been convicted of anything, George was still eager to make amends. He'd recruited Bailey to play secret Santa. As word spread, the townsfolk's anger lessened. His inspiring gesture set off a wave of goodwill, thawing the chill that had settled over Sweetwater Springs.

However, the incident sparked a concentrated investigation into the town's financial history. George had revealed that his great-uncle's records uncovered a troubling pattern of unusual transactions dating back to the 1950s.

Who might the embezzler possibly be? A descendant of the original Sweetwater family? With no one remaining, the theory quickly unraveled.

Or someone entirely different?

Once again, Emma and Victor put their detective skills to the test in the storage room of the bakery.

A couple of evenings later, they sifted through a collection of clues, their lively debate tapering off. Victor's expression shifted, his gaze pulling from the papers to the window as if searching for the right words.

Emma detected the change immediately. "What's wrong?" she asked.

For several seconds, he didn't respond. Then he turned, his eyes meeting hers. "I received a job offer," he said quietly. "A significant one. With the FBI in Washington, DC."

Her heart jolted. She forced a small smile, a knot of dread tangling with the hope lodged deep in her chest. "I guess they don't need agents in Italy."

"No," he replied.

Not as far as Europe, but still ... D.C. was almost three

thousand miles away, on the opposite coast. The distance hit Emma like a sudden drop, leaving her struggling to keep her emotions in check. A quick math estimate told her it would typically take around 40-45 hours of continuous driving, not accounting for stops, rest, or traffic.

Her smile faltered. She forced it into place. "I didn't realize you were looking. You've got your inheritance, so …" She hesitated. "You don't really need to work, right?"

"I sent out a few applications before leaving Venice," he admitted, his shoulders lifting in a casual shrug. "I've always believed that a job provides you with something that money can't buy. Purpose. Growth. Plus, it's a field I care about."

Emma's heart sank a little more. "That's … that's great, Victor." She swallowed hard, the words tasting like ash, each word harder to get out than the last. "When do you leave?"

He reached for her hands. "That's the thing. I don't know if I want to. Sweetwater Springs—isn't another assignment for me. It's developed into something more."

"Home." A lump formed in her throat as she battled the rising tide of emotions.

"And you … you've become …" He trailed off, the unspoken words hanging between them, filling her with both fear and longing.

Her mind spun, a torrent of beliefs crashing together. She couldn't allow herself to believe their relationship was what she'd waited for. Not yet. Not when everything was slipping away. The thought of losing him, just as she was opening her heart again, was devastating.

"You should take the job." Her voice trembled; the words hollow. She pulled her hands free from his, feeling the sudden absence of warmth.

"I haven't decided anything." His tone was tender but stable, as if trying to tether them to something steady. "I wanted to talk to you first."

"There's nothing to talk about." She turned away, her breath catching as she blinked back tears that threatened to spill. "You should go."

Everyone leaves in the end.

An abrupt crash from the street snapped them out of their intense discussion, and they rushed to the window. Snowflake darted by, something gleaming clenched between her teeth. Behind her, Delilah gave chase, tinsel streaming from her coat. The ridiculous sight almost made Emma laugh—if only her heart wasn't breaking.

"Is that …?" Emma squinted, the image briefly pulling her out of the storm of emotions.

"The missing silver star from the town's Christmas tree," Victor confirmed.

"The star had disappeared?" Emma grabbed her parka and scrambled after him.

"Yes. People were talking about it in the bakery yesterday," he said, holding the door open for her.

Blissful Bites had reopened with limited hours, and to Emma's relief, the first few days were promising. She'd started stepping out of the cocoon she had built around herself, little by little. But when she tallied up the receipts, the initial glimmer of hope dimmed. The numbers were clear and unforgiving. Bills for ingredients, utilities, and the upcoming mortgage crowded her thoughts, reminding her how precarious everything was.

Her gaze flicked to the HELP WANTED sign she'd propped on a shelf. In her bakery, she needed extra hands more than ever, but the question was whether she had the means to afford it. The endless worry gnawed at her, a silent companion refusing to be shaken.

She pushed those thoughts aside, focusing on the chase. She and Victor followed Snowflake's erratic path as the kitten led them on a whimsical dance—darting into alleys, squeezing under parked cars. They kept pace, always a step behind, until Snowflake disappeared into an overgrown garden by the town hall.

Victor lunged for Snowflake's collar, his fingers missing the tag as the kitten darted away. "Where did she go—"

Suddenly, he stopped.

Emma peered over his shoulder. "What is it?"

He brushed aside more foliage to reveal what lay hidden. "Stone steps … leading down," he said, a note of surprise in his voice. The staircase spiraled deep into the earth, with only faint light filtering through. From below came a soft, insistent mew.

"Snowflake?" Emma called.

A flash of white darted beneath them—Snowflake's tail flickering around a bend.

"There she is!" Victor ducked his head, the narrow ceiling forcing him to hunch over. "Careful," he added, voice low. "The passage tightens as we go."

They descended quickly, the space closing in, their footsteps resounding through the tunnel. The rough-hewn walls squeezed them into a single file, cobwebs grazing their skin as they hurried after the pattering of tiny paws.

The staircase wound deeper.

"I've never seen this on any town map," she murmured, testing each step with a cautious foot. She half-expected them to give under her weight, though they held firm.

Victor pulled out his phone, switching on its flashlight. "That's because this staircase shouldn't exist. The area was meant to be filled in decades ago—around the same time they decommissioned old storm cellars."

They groped their way further; the passage stretching endlessly. Beams of light from Victor's phone flew across the walls, flickering off ancient stones.

At last, the staircase gave way to a corridor, its low ceiling barely high enough for them to stand upright. The walls pressed close, the air thick with the scent of damp earth.

Watch your step," Victor warned. "I remember reading about these in the historical records, but I assumed they were all sealed off."

Emma glanced around. "This is more than a cellar. These are tunnels."

The passage widened abruptly, opening into a circular chamber. Victor's flashlight beam revealed dust-covered shelves lined with the remnants of long-abandoned civil defense supplies. Most were bare, save for a few sagging cardboard boxes and a stack of rusting folding chairs.

What caught Emma's attention wasn't the shelves or their contents. In the center of the room stood a large stone pedestal, worn smooth from what appeared to be decades of wear.

"This is no ordinary chamber," she breathed, moving closer to examine the pedestal. Faint patterns covered its surface, swirling designs that shimmered in the flashlight's beam.

"The town's idea of an impromptu storage solution." Victor crouched beside it, running his hand along the edge.

"Why would anyone bring an object like this here?" Emma asked.

He snapped a photo. "There were rumors, stories about tunnels, secret passageways the founding families used. Nothing about this."

Emma's fingertips hit a ridge in the stone. "Wait—there's more." She pressed down, revealing a hidden compartment beneath.

She pulled out a metal box and pried it open.

Victor's flashlight illuminated the contents inside: yellowed documents, faded photographs, and a carefully folded map of Sweetwater Springs.

"These must be decades old," she whispered, almost afraid to breathe too hard for fear the papers might disintegrate.

Victor lifted several. "Correspondence between the founding families," he murmured, reading the faded ink. "And financial records dating back to the early days of Sweetwater Springs."

As they leafed through the papers, a story took shape—of the town's initial struggles, covert deals made in shadows, and long-buried secrets kept out of the public eye.

Emma's gaze locked on one particular entry. "Victor," she said, her voice wavering slightly, "these withdrawals are all authorized by Gus Stratton."

Victor's silence spoke volumes, heavy with disbelief. When he finally responded, his words were guarded. "Are you certain?"

"It's plainly written in ink," she replied, a burden of phrases she was reluctant to speak aloud. "Gus is an ally. Why would he—"

Victor straightened. "We're missing something. Context, motive, explanation— there are too many unknowns, and Gus wouldn't betray the town. There must be a reason."

"I hope you're right, but we can't ignore this either."

"We won't," he said. "We'll investigate discreetly without tipping anyone off."

They shifted their attention back to the pages. Even the most trusted figures appeared to harbor uncertainty. The more they explored, the more intricate the story became.

Victor's flashlight flickered, catching on a glinting object a few inches beyond them. He crouched, brushing away dust and dirt, then lifted a lockbox, its brass corners dulled with age.

He opened it and inhaled sharply. Stacks of neatly folded checks sat next to meticulously kept ledgers, their pages filled with careful notations—dates, amounts, and signatures.

"Stolen," Emma murmured.

Victor stood, staring at the contents of the box, the implications swirling between them. "These tunnels probably connect the major buildings in town—City Hall, the bank, even the courthouse. They had the ability to shift funds and documents without being noticed for many years. No wonder people never detected it. They had a seamless cover."

Who were they?

The quiet amplified Emma's thoughts. This discovery went beyond simple secrets; it was the means to unscrambling the town's long-buried corruption.

However, what pressed heavier was the realization that someone as trusted as Gus Stratton was involved. The town she recognized had more than its charm—it had a hidden underbelly, stretching back generations.

"To think," she mused, "these tunnels were most likely built for the town's protection. How ironic that they were used to undermine it instead."

Victor tucked the box under his arm, his jaw set. "We'll keep this quiet until we know more. If Gus is involved … we can't let anyone find out until we have all the facts."

"The lighthouse." Emma indicated a marking on the map. "Exactly where we found those ruins by the lake."

Victor nodded. "Emma, this could be the key to the town's financial struggles."

"I hope we're not stirring up more trouble than we can handle."

As if in response to her unease, Victor's phone pinged. He scowled at the screen.

"What is it?" she asked.

"A tip. There are several discrepancies in the library's budget." His eyes locked with hers. "I'll look into it tomorrow."

Emma's heart sank, a hollow sensation robbing her of

breath. The library. Nora's library. Could her dear friend truly have gotten caught up in this twisted mess? The possibility seemed unthinkable, yet the evidence was slowly closing in.

Before she expressed her concerns, a familiar voice sounded. Quickly, Victor set the box behind him.

"Well, sugar plums," Delilah's tone faltered, her usual light cadence hitching mid-sentence, as she appeared at the top of the stairs. "Our Snowflake has quite the nose for secrets." She indicated the kitten, perched atop a pile of papers, the missing star beside her.

Delilah descended the stairs, her eyes flitting between Emma and Victor, clearly piecing together the tension. "I was chasing Snowflake." She glanced around, taking in the remnants of the past littering the space. "Seems like you two have uncovered more than a Christmas star."

Emma forced a smile, thinking of Gus, and how his possible guilt would affect Delilah. "It's … complicated," she said.

Delilah's attention returned to Snowflake. "My little rascal has a knack for finding what's lost."

Emma met Victor's gaze. He shifted, standing in front of the lockbox, as if to signal their next move.

"Secrets have a way of crawling out of the shadows when you least expect them," Delilah added, her words laced with both humor and a hint of darkness.

Emma's stomach twisted uneasily. Delilah was right—this discovery was only the beginning.

CHAPTER 11

The next morning, Emma arrived at the bakery early, her nerves on edge. Sleep had been a distant dream, her mind spinning with worries about Nora's connection to the embezzlement case.

Victor was already at the bakery, relief clear on his face.

"False alarm," he said as soon as she spotted him. "It was an accounting error. Nora was the one who spotted it and flagged it for review."

Emma slumped against the door, her body releasing the tension that had gripped her for hours. "Thank goodness. I don't know what I would've done if—"

"It's a good thing," he assured her. "It shows the system is working. People are paying attention."

She nodded, the knot in her chest finally loosening. Yet a quiet voice in the back of her mind warned her that next time, they might not be so lucky. How many more twists did this investigation hold?

Over the following days, the townspeople explored the hidden network of the storm cellar, creating a whirlwind of activity. With each discovery, pieces of forgotten history came to light—love letters between star-crossed lovers, records of secret acts of kindness, and, yes, evidence of long-standing wrongs.

Rather than tearing the community apart, these revelations brought the folks closer together. People owned their past mistakes, determined to build a better tomorrow.

Victor stood at the edge of the square, observing the holiday commotion with a mingling of admiration and uncertainty. He'd come to Sweetwater Springs to investigate missing funds that could threaten the town's future. What he'd found was a community wrapped in history, secrets, and deep ties that no ledger could capture.

As families admired the shop windows, each display more dazzling than the last, Victor smiled. Sweetwater Springs had an infectious spirit, making his investigation both harder and more rewarding than he had imagined.

His eyes found Emma across the square, helping a group of preschoolers hang ornaments on the town's Christmas tree. The sound of her laughter reached him, stirring something deep inside—a longing for a connection he hadn't realized he missed.

He sighed. The case was far from solved, and his time in Sweetwater Springs was temporary. But as the holiday magic seeped into his heart, he questioned what truly mattered—solving a financial mystery or being part of a greater cause—like the surrounding community.

Emma waved at him, and he grinned, waving back.

This place embraced the holidays with unbridled enthusiasm. Every shop window tried to outshine the next, each more elaborate than the last.

Victor peeked into the historical society, where a vintage horse-drawn sleigh, polished and gleaming, took center stage in the lobby. It overflowed with donated gifts, and schoolchildren crowded around, eager to add their wrapped packages.

Victor had gotten to know some of these kids through the children's choir. Little Jamie, struggling to carry a box almost as big as he was, beamed with pride as he placed it among the others. Reserved Sarah edged forward to lay her handmade card on top of the presents. The volunteers smiled, touched by the pure generosity.

Meanwhile, most of the time Emma was in full baking mode, the smell of anise and peppermint drifting from her bakery, drawing passersby in. Even Mr. Finch, notorious for his "Bah, humbug!" attitude, surprised everyone by offering his yard for a pop-up hot chocolate stand to raise money for the animal shelter.

Though the Holiday Market had ended, the square had transformed into a festive bazaar. Booths, designed like gingerbread houses, were bursting with handmade crafts. The mouth-watering aromas of sizzling meats, caramelized onions, and roasted garlic from food trucks scented the air. The crunch of frost-covered grass mixed with the rich scent of fresh coffee, and now and then, the aroma of wood-fired pizzas cut through the savory smoke from the barbecue.

Teenagers clustered around a storyteller spinning tales of Arctic adventures, while their parents debated the merits of various Christmas tree varieties.

As dusk settled, a winter mist crept through the town, muffling sounds and softening edges. Carolers, huddled under a shop awning, harmonized to *The Huron Carol*. Strings of golden bulbs draped between lampposts, their glow reflecting off slick cobblestones and creating the illusion of a path of stars.

Victor, somehow, had found himself at the heart of all this—helping to piece together the town's history, while trying to make sense of his own life. Despite all his travels and never staying in one place for long, Sweetwater Springs had a way of drawing him in, making him wonder how he—a wanderer—ended up in a town so rooted in tradition.

And through it all, Emma was there. Constant, and always by his side.

As Christmas Eve drew near, the townsfolk gathered for the children's choir performance. Families bundled in thick wool scarves, clutching steaming thermoses of tea and hot apple cider. Soon, candles tucked into paper bags would flicker in the sharp night air as the sun dipped beyond the trees.

Mayor Thompson climbed onto a small stage, quickly assembled for the event. Its wooden planks, slightly worn but sturdy, were raised a few feet above the ground. Volunteers draped simple string lights along the edges. A backdrop of painted canvas depicting the town's familiar skyline fluttered in the breeze. Special guests were provided with a few folding chairs arranged neatly in front.

Normally cheerful, tonight the mayor tugged at his collar as if he were uncomfortable. The gathering quieted as he approached the microphone. To the side, the children's choir fidgeted, their breaths rising in tiny clouds.

"Friends," Mayor Thompson started, his voice carrying easily over the square. "This holiday season has brought more than cheer. We've come face to face with our past—the good and the bad." He scanned the people—some concerned, others curious, all attentive. "Tonight, as we prepare for Christmas, let's take this walk to heal, to forgive, and to build a better future."

He motioned to Emma and Victor, standing hand in hand. "Because of these two, and many of you, we can set things right. To honor our past while building something brand new."

As if orchestrated by an unseen hand, the festive tree in the square blinked to life. Each decoration suggested stories long forgotten, the struggles and victories that had shaped them all. At the very top, a star glittered, bright and clear. It was the same star that Snowflake had led Emma and Victor to find. A symbol of serendipity and the unexpected paths that lead to truth.

Emma looked up at Victor. The radiance of a thousand twinkling lights shone in her eyes, transforming them into pools of dazzling blue. There was an intensity there, a depth of emotions. She was a vision of winter elegance, wrapped in a deep burgundy wool coat that hugged her curves. She artfully draped a cream-colored scarf, with delicate snowflake embroidery, around her neck. Her blonde hair cascaded in silky waves from beneath a matching burgundy beret.

"We were meant to find that star," she said.

Victor smiled, brushing a loose strand of hair from her face. "You're right," he whispered. Despite the chill in the air, her warmth made the cold seem distant.

He couldn't help feeling self-conscious, and a tad under-dressed for the occasion. A charcoal gray peacoat with a holiday-green sweater beneath was his choice, paired with dark jeans and polished brown boots. He swept a hand through his hair; the evening breeze having left it more than a bit unruly.

"Emma," he murmured, surprised at the roughness in his voice. He led her away from the crowd, creating a small world for the two of them. "Watching you these past weeks— how determined you've been, how much you've grown—has made me realize something,"

"What?" The pride and wonder etched on her face stirred

a sensation deep within him. In one beat, his impending decision bore down relentlessly, whether to take the job or stay in Sweetwater Springs, and the decision seemed both monumental and inconsequential. Washington represented everything he wanted—prestige, challenge, and a chance to make a real difference. The job represented the achievement of years of effort and ambition, a significant opportunity that aligned with his determined, unsettled lifestyle.

However, Sweetwater Springs was changing him. A sensation tugged—a connection to the town, the people, his family relation to Elliot and Delilah. For the first time, the idea of home meant more than a temporary stop. The town gave off a sense of wellbeing, unlike any other place. The ties bore a striking disparity to the nomadic, often lonely childhood he'd experienced.

And then, most importantly, there was her. Emma.

His eyes traced her features, capturing each detail. She represented everything he loved about this community—her strength, her kindness, her beauty. Seeing her push through her own fears had inspired him in ways he hadn't expected.

Could anything in D.C. compare to what he'd found? A job was merely a job, but here … here there was romance, family, and a future he hadn't ever dared to dream about.

Emma's gaze met his, tiny beads of moisture catching on her lashes.

His heart surged. Maybe the choice wasn't about a career at all, but about finding where he truly belonged.

"What did you realize?" she repeated, her voice soft but insistent.

Victor took a breath, his emotions too tangled to express in words. "This," he whispered, bending to kiss her.

As their lips touched, everything disappeared. The noise of the crowd blurred into a faint hum, leaving only the two of them—her hands in his. The kiss was both tender and passionate, a culmination of attraction that had been building between them for weeks. Victor poured his feelings into it—his gratitude for her thoughtfulness, and the love that had quietly grown day by day.

When they finally pulled apart, reality crept back in. He noted the indulgent gasps and murmurs from the people nearby, and he couldn't bring himself to care. All that mattered was Emma.

The children's choir began to sing *Silent Night*, their voices rising sweetly. The song floated over the square, adding a layer of magic to the already enchanted evening.

He took in the scene—the twinkling ice crystals on the leaves, the hushed whisper of snowflakes falling, the friends sharing the moment. It was so different from the impersonal winters he'd known, where the chill seemed to push people apart, not bring them together.

His breath fogged in the cold air, but something caught his eye—a shadow moving at the edge of the crowd. The figure glided quickly. For a second, Victor's instincts kicked in.

A man. And the man strode with intent. What was he doing?

As swiftly as the question appeared, it faded. Tonight wasn't about chasing shadows. It was about belonging.

Victor wrapped his arm around Emma as they listened to the choir. The children's angelic voices filled the night, and for the first time, he knew a sense of calm.

With this beautiful woman by his side and the magic of Christmas surrounding them, he hoped that whatever choice he made, it would be the right one.

CHAPTER 12

*E*mma burst into the bakery's back room. She and Victor had hurried back for some last-minute details while Nora read *'Twas the Night Before Christmas* to the crowd. That, Emma knew, would be followed by an ugly sweater contest, with small prizes awarded to the winners.

As usual, Victor was engrossed in the ledgers in front of him.

"I've figured it out!" she exclaimed.

He looked up. "Figured out what?"

"About Gus!" She spread out a couple of documents she had printed. "I looked over the town council minutes. Turns out there was a scholarship fund set up for Gus's late wife's memory. He's been managing it all these years."

"What about the withdrawals?"

"They match the scholarship disbursements exactly. The dates and amounts line up."

"Shows how complex this whole situation is." Victor let out a relieved sigh. "I'm so glad we didn't confront Gus about this."

Emma nodded. "Me, too."

They quicly put the finishing touches on a display of gingerbread lighthouses in the window. Each was a miniature replica of the rediscovered beacon, complete with tiny sugar windows that refracted the streetlamps. Microscopic LED bulbs, cleverly hidden within the structures, pulsed, mimicking the rhythm of a real lighthouse's rotating beam.

Emma twisted to admire their craftsmanship. Victor stood beside her, his arm resting casually around her waist.

"They're beautiful," he said. "But not as beautiful as you."

"Thank you." Her cheeks warmed. "Do you think the kids will like them?"

"Are you kidding? They'll love them. Though I bet Delilah won't allow them to eat any. She can't handle another sugar high for any little ones. Besides, it's Christmas Eve, and many folks are planning to attend church service. They need to be attentive for Pastor David's sermon."

Right on cue, Delilah appeared, and Snowflake perched on her shoulder like a furry epaulette. The kitten had become the unofficial mascot of the Luminary Walk, her white fur decorated with a petite strand of battery-operated lights.

"Ready, sugar plum?" Delilah inquired.

Emma nodded and took a deep breath, nerves fluttering in her chest. The organizers had invited her and Victor to lead the walk, sharing the history of the town's founding and the rediscovery of the lighthouse. Though a tremendous honor—it was also a tad intimidating.

"You've got this," Victor whispered.

Once they reached the square, paper lanterns were lit, their flickering lights turning frost-kissed streets into a carpet of diamonds. The village stirred, itching to start their yearly evening march.

Emma took the initiative. "Friends," she began, surprising herself with how calm she sounded. "Tonight, we're not only rejoicing in Christmas. We're celebrating the resiliency of Sweetwater Springs."

She motioned toward the park, where the remnants of the lighthouse stood. "As the star that guided the wise men, our lighthouse has steered us back to the heart of our town."

She led the crowd through the streets, stopping at key locations. Indicating the location of the old mill on the outskirts, she recounted stories of the people who had outdone themselves to preserve the town's history. In the park, she revealed the true origins of the beloved carousel, a gift from a repentant con man who'd found redemption in Sweetwater Springs.

Finally, they reached the historical society, where Gus Stratton and Daniel Whitfield had placed a beautifully decorated sleigh. Lanterns bathed the sleigh's polished edges in a subtle radiance.

Emma smiled. "This, as you all know, is our Giving Sleigh, a symbol of the generosity that defines us."

The antique sleigh, lovingly restored to its former glory, gleamed. The cherry-wood frame bore elaborate carvings of holly and ivy, while the runners, coated in a lustrous gold, shimmered with promise.

Mounds of red and green foil-wrapped presents spilled over the sides. Plush teddy bears peeked out between the boxes tied with satin ribbons, while activity sets and children's books teetered on top. Brand new wool coats were casually draped over the back, their heavy fabric inviting warmth.

Wicker baskets brimming with groceries lined the floor of the sleigh—jars of homemade jam snuggled against cookie tins, while bags of fresh produce peeked out from packages of pasta and canned goods.

Emma stood straighter. "This is more than a collection of

gifts. This reflects our spirit. Every donation, every offering, represents the love and care we share with one another."

"What started as a simple idea has grown into a truly remarkable event," Victor said. "Tomorrow morning, these offerings will bring joy to families here, and to the neighboring communities as well."

Emma swallowed a lump in her throat. In the past several months, parting with even the smallest of items had been hard for her. Hoarding had become a way to hold on to memories, to keep loss at bay. But everything had changed. In the town's embrace, she found the courage to speak.

"I'd like to share a personal story." A shaky exhale escaped her lips. "Losing people makes us cling to what's left, doesn't it? Objects become stand-ins for the love we've lost. For me, it was month-old newspapers, chipped mugs, even perfume bottles long emptied. Each held a memory I couldn't bear to lose."

She paused, meeting Victor's gaze. His steadiness gave her the strength to continue.

"This December, I realized something," she said, her voice growing stronger. "The real treasures aren't items gathering dust on a shelf. They're the moments we share, the laughter that fills this square, and the way we come together when it matters most. To release the past is not about loss—rather, it's making room for recent memories, new joys."

She gestured to the sleigh. "Every gift is special. This is an opportunity to remind someone that they're not alone, that they matter. The Giving Sleigh is about opening our hearts and recognizing that true wealth isn't in what we keep. True wealth is in the love we share."

"Bravo!" Delilah called out, resulting in a wave of applause.

Emma beamed. This tradition, this moment, represented

a return to where it all began. She had faced her fears and turned her past pain into strength.

She reached into her satchel and drew out an ornate wooden box, its edges worn smooth from decades of use. "This jewelry box belonged to my grandmother," she said.

She placed it in the sleigh, her fingers lingering on the familiar wood. "For years, I never opened it. Now I understand that the real value isn't in the gemstones inside. The significance lies in the memories it holds."

Upon opening the lid, she revealed vintage pieces cushioned on worn velvet. "Each item in here has a story about my grandmother—a first date, an anniversary, a cherished friendship. I'm also including something special: my grandmother's snickerdoodle recipe. This is the specific one she taught me as a little girl. We burned more batches than I care to admit, but eventually, I got it right."

She swiped at her eyes, wet with unshed tears. "I hope whoever receives this finds as much delight and satisfaction in it as I have. Maybe they'll wear the jewelry and create distinct memories, or bake those cookies and start their own family traditions. Either way, I believe sharing it will bring more happiness than holding onto it ever could."

As Emma closed the lid, the quiet *click* resonated in the still air, symbolizing not only the closing of a box, but the dawn of the next chapter—one of release and renewal.

James McAllister jostled his way to the front. He'd carefully styled his auburn hair, despite not completely hiding the retreating hairline. Emma had seen little of him in town, probably because of the demands of his shop, *McAllister's Game Haven*. He was busy; she supposed.

His blue eyes swept over her, sharp and calculating. The smile he offered seemed polite enough, though it never quite reached his piercing eyes. The last few times they had crossed paths, Emma couldn't pinpoint it exactly, but he'd left her with an uneasy feeling.

"This is all truly inspiring," he said, his voice carrying an edge of unease. "Given the town's recent … financial concerns, how uplifting to see everyone coming together." He paused, glancing around as though gauging the crowd's reaction. "I'm interested in contributing as well." He placed a stack of board games into the sleigh, his hands holding onto the boxes a second too long.

At the mention of the town's financial troubles, a murmur rippled through the gathering. The mysterious discrepancies in Sweetwater Springs' accounts had everyone whispering about possible embezzlement, though for these few hours, the spirit of giving had overshadowed those concerns.

"Where are your parents?" Emma asked, hoping to steer the conversation away from the tension. "They always attend the Luminary Walk, but I haven't seen them tonight."

James's lips twitched into a half-smile. "Oh, you know how it is with the elderly," he said, his tone light but dismissive. "They're probably at home, arguing over which Christmas special to watch. Dad is stuck on *It's a Wonderful Life*, while Mom insists on *Miracle on 34th Street*. I told them I'd represent the McAllister spirit of generosity." He waved a hand, as if brushing off any further questions about their absence.

Emma's stomach twisted. The elder McAllisters were pillars of the community, their benevolence extending far beyond Christmas traditions. They'd tirelessly supported James, especially during his rebellious teenage years. His flippant tone didn't sit right with her, though she stayed silent. She'd make a point to check on them soon.

Delilah sidled up, her holiday sweater so outrageous it practically jingled with festive cheer. Tinsel trimmed the collar, tiny ornaments dangled from the sleeves, and a battery-powered Santa let out a tinny "Ho ho ho!" every time she moved. At her feet, Snowflake pranced around, looking half adorable, half annoyed.

Gus hovered near her; his usual stoic expression softened by the reindeer antlers perched at an awkward angle on his head. He gave Emma a wry grin and mouthed, "Delilah's idea." Then he nodded approvingly as Delilah rested a hand on Emma's shoulder.

"You've given this town more than cookies and pastries," Delilah said, her sweater offering another "Ho ho ho!" as she shifted, causing Snowflake to scamper behind Gus's legs. "The reminder of the spirit of Christmas is everywhere."

People stepped forward, contributing their own last-minute donations to the sleigh. Olivia and Daniel Whitfield contributed a set of children's books, while Elliot and Nora added a handful of grocery store gift cards.

Soon, Lillian and Theodore Weatherly navigated forward. Lillian, despite a recent illness, was the picture of grace in her tailored cashmere coat, a string of pearls resting elegantly at her throat. Theodore, his arm protectively around his wife, carried a finely wrapped package.

With a tap of his cane, Theodore began, "If I may, I would love to share a verse for the occasion." The gathering hushed as he recited:

"In giving, we receive a greater gift,
Our hearts, like this sleigh, overflow with grace.
Each act of kindness helps to heal a rift,
And imparts a smile to every waiting face."

Lillian beamed at her husband, then turned to Emma. "My dear," she said, her voice tender yet resolute, "Theodore and I want to donate this." She gestured to the package in his hands. "This book is a first edition of *A Christmas Carol*. We hope it brings as much inspiration to the recipient as it has to us."

While Theodore placed the book in the sleigh, Lillian continued, "We've included a note about our literary circle. There's no expiration date on the joy of reading together." She glanced at Nora, the town's beloved librarian. "Isn't that right, Nora?"

Nora dipped her head in agreement. "Right."

As the crowd dispersed to continue the Luminary Walk, Victor nestled Emma closer. "I'm proud of you," he whispered.

She angled nearer and grinned. "Thank you."

The act of giving away a cherished possession had brought her an unexpected gift. She had gained far more valuable rewards—fitting into the community and being part of a greater purpose.

While they walked, the streets came alive in a new way. Neighbors who had lived side by side for years seemed to see one another with fresh eyes, a deeper bond taking root, tied to the town's shared history.

But the evening held an unexpected surprise.

Emma led the group through the park, their footsteps crackling on the frosty grass. They stopped by the lake, its tranquil surface reflecting the light of the moon.

"I'd like to introduce a remarkable individual," Emma said, her voice resonating with clarity in the darkness. "Someone with ancestors in Sweetwater Springs since the very beginning."

Martha Sweetwater, a distant cousin of the town's founding family, advanced to the front to stand near Emma. She had left the town decades ago. Now, here she was, returning at the most unexpected moment.

Despite her years, Martha bore her age with refinement, her silver hair styled in neat waves under a vintage hat. She leaned lightly on a polished cane, taking in the crowd.

A ripple of whispered recognition spread through the older townsfolk.

"Martha?" Theodore Weatherly's voice broke through the chatter. "Hasn't it been years since—"

"Since the centennial celebration, Theodore," she finished. "I decided it was time to come home, especially after hearing about all the excitement lately."

The embezzled funds came to mind, despite no one voicing the subject.

Martha gestured toward the lake, its inky waters stretching beneath a thin veil of mist. "There have always been stories about the town founders," she stated. "Yes, they were eccentric, although their quirks were more than odd street names. They loved their puzzles and riddles, and they embedded them right into the town's design."

From her purse, she pulled out a vintage map and passed it to Emma. "This is Sweetwater Springs as it was first laid out. Look closely."

Emma unfolded the edges and peered at the map before handing it to Victor. The streets formed a curious maze when viewed from above. Victor studied it, then passed it along to Theodore, who nodded.

"I've often wondered about the peculiar intersection of Riddle Lane and Enigma Avenue," Theodore mused. "Seems our ancestors had quite a sense of humor."

"Or perhaps they were leaving us clues, breadcrumbs to follow," Martha said. "Sweetwater Springs has always had its share of secrets and revelations."

True. There was something magical about discovering a town's hidden lore, especially on a night like Christmas Eve.

As Martha shared more descriptions, Victor whispered in Emma's ear. "You've succeeded. You've brought everyone together."

"We've succeeded," she corrected. "I couldn't have done any of this without you."

Soon, the Luminary Walk developed into an impromptu celebration by the lake. Delilah strummed the first notes of *Away in a Manger* on her ukulele. Her voice, though out of tune, was clear. Several joined in, blending into the lively chorus of *Jingle Bells*.

O Holy Night followed, drawing more people. As the music continued, Olivia served cups of rich, hot cocoa from a pop-up stand, the scent of chocolate and cinnamon mingling with the pine-scented breeze.

Meanwhile, Elliot and Nora moved through the gathering, their arms laden with heavy wool scarves. "Even though she isn't here tonight, these are from Mrs. McAllister's knitting circle," Elliot explained, draping a lime-green creation around an elderly man's shoulders. Nora handed a vibrant red scarf to a young mother, adding, "The ladies have been working on these since August, if you can believe it."

Near midnight, as the festivities quieted, and several people headed to church, Emma and Victor returned to her bakery. Moonlight glinted off the frosted windowpanes, and she removed her gloves to clear the glass.

When she reached for her keys, Victor's hand covered hers.

"Not yet," he said. "I have a surprise for you."

He led her around to the back of the shop, where a modest vegetable garden lay hushed under a thin blanket of snow. Gnarled apple trees, their trunks damp from winter rain, stretched their branches toward a star-studded sky. In the center of the garden stood a wrought-iron table, a secluded island in the serene embrace of winter.

"Victor," she murmured, her voice barely more than a breath. "What's all this?"

In the moonlight, the scene resembled a vision out of a

dream—two elegant place settings, delicate china, insulated ceramic mugs, and polished silver. Beside Emma's plate sat a box wrapped in deep velvet. A thermos of steaming hot cider gave off a spicy fragrance, accompanied by gingerbread biscuits dusted with powdered sugar.

Victor pulled out her chair, the metal legs scraping against the frozen ground.

"With all the excitement, we haven't had many proper dates," he said.

Her eyes never left his face. "You figured that Christmas Eve was the perfect time?"

"Absolutely." He settled in the seat opposite her and reached over the table to take her hands. "These past weeks have been the most exciting, terrifying, and wonderful of my life. And I realized why. It's all because of you."

He drew a deep breath that misted in the cold air. "We haven't known each other long, but I've never been more certain of anything. I love you, Emma Jacobsen. No matter what happens, I want you to know that."

His words washed over her.

Endearments were sweet, although it was the actions behind them that spoke the loudest. Still, she couldn't help the way her heart expanded. Victor was here. She wasn't spending Christmas Eve alone.

She stared at the velvet box, her attention captured as if drawn by an invisible force. "You did all this? When?"

"Oh." He chuckled. "Elliot and Nora pitched in. Romantics, those two, especially now that they're married." He nodded toward the box. "Aren't you going to open my gift?"

"Yes. Of course." Her breath hitched, her fingers gliding over the plush velvet. Slowly, she revealed a delicate silver charm bracelet nestled inside. The bracelet featured a single, beautifully crafted charm—a tiny lighthouse, engraved with fine details that captured its essence of guidance and hope. A symbol of the connection they had found in Sweetwater Springs, of light shining in the darkest places.

"Merry Christmas, Raindrop," he murmured, bending in to press his lips against hers.

"Thank you, Victor. Merry Christmas."

The distant church bells chimed, heralding Christmas.

Surrounded by the silent beauty of the winter garden, she had discovered a truth far more precious than any treasure.

She was in love with Victor Steele.

HOURS AFTERWARD, as the excitement of the previous evening faded and Christmas morning dawned, Emma swung her legs out of bed, shivering as her bare feet touched the cold wooden floor. She rubbed the sleep from her eyes, padded to the window, and peered out. Main Street lay deserted, a ribbon of white under the inky sky. A thin layer of snow blanketed parked cars, and the sidewalks were unmarred by footprints. Dark storefronts held silent; their CLOSED signs scarcely visible behind icy panes. Only the distant hum of a lone plow broke the pre-dawn stillness.

She stood in her living room, taking in the transformation. Where she had once cluttered every surface with trinkets and mementos, there was a sense of calm. She had tastefully decorated her Christmas tree with a few carefully chosen decorations, each holding a special meaning.

She stepped to the kitchen and ran her hand along the clear counter. Though it hadn't been easy, Victor's support and her friends' encouragement had helped her make significant progress in releasing what she no longer needed. The journey of uncovering Sweetwater Springs' history had taught her that memories didn't live in things—they lived in the heart.

She showered and dressed in jeans and a festive red

sweater, then turned her attention to wrapping Victor's Christmas gift. She carefully folded shiny gold paper around a square box, her fingers moving with precision. Inside was an antique camera she'd found at Mr. Garrison's shop. A beautifully preserved Leica from the 1950s, its metal body showed enough wear to hint at the stories it had taken.

She had observed Victor's interest in photography during their adventures, often seeing him frame a shot with his smartphone.

This camera seemed perfect—a bridge between his modern tech background and Sweetwater Springs abundant history. She included a roll of film and a note about the local developer who could process the film, imagining the moments Victor might take photographs of the town and their time together.

She tied a red velvet ribbon around the package, then hesitated. Was it too impersonal? Did it strike the right balance for their budding relationship?

Her hand naturally gravitated to the bracelet she wore, reminding her of the profound meaning in a simple gift.

She placed his present on her dresser and shook off any doubts. She needed to prepare baked goods for the Christmas meal at the homeless shelter. With that, she headed downstairs to the bakery, where the scent of yeast and sugar greeted her like an old friend.

Tying on her apron, she got to work, her hands gliding with practiced efficiency as she kneaded dough for cinnamon rolls and shaped loaves of bread. Today wasn't about presents or grand gestures. Today was about being with the people she cared about and giving back to the community that had given her so much.

She checked her watch. In a few hours, she and Victor would join the crowd at the little white church. Pastor David always had a way of lifting spirits. Afterward, they'd head to the shelter to dish out roasted turkey and Christmas cheer.

Victor.

Emma struggled to take a full breath. His job prospect in Washington hovered in her thoughts, darkening the fragile happiness they'd built. Would their connection survive the distance if he accepted the offer? Would she end up watching another person she cared for slip from her life?

She pressed her fingers to her forehead, trying to dislodge the doubts.

The shelter was counting on her, and she wouldn't allow personal worries to affect her contributions to the community. Still, as she began wrapping the cooled rolls, a profound sense of uncertainty settled in her chest.

This Christmas might be the first and last one she and Victor might ever spend together in her beloved hometown.

CHAPTER 13

The day after Christmas, Sweetwater Springs exhaled. The whirlwind of festive preparations and heartfelt moments gave way to cozy contentment, as if the town itself cherished the afterglow of the celebration.

Emma settled in her bakery, surveying the remnants of holiday cheer. She wore a blue knit dress, its soft wool shielding her from the persistent chill. Opaque black tights and practical flats provided comfort with a hint of post-seasonal polish, while she tied her hair back in a messy bun under a hairnet. Flour dust clung to her seasoned apron like a badge of honor, evidence of the morning's work.

The bakery was open, though foot traffic was light; most of the townsfolk remained nestled at home, savoring left-overs and enjoying their new gifts.

Her thoughts drifted to the previous evening and the excitement on Victor's face when he unwrapped the vintage Leica camera. His eyes lit with boyish enthusiasm as he turned the camera over in his hands, admiring the slight wear on its metal body. "Emma, this is incredible!" he had exclaimed. "This beauty must've taken a ton of gorgeous photos in its day."

He spent the rest of the night fiddling with the camera, capturing candid shots of her giggles as she tried to dodge his lens. The last photo he took of them together—heads bent close, smiles wide—was a textbook start to the camera's next phase.

The bakery was quiet, a glaring difference to the laughter that had filled it hours before, though she assumed the day held its own adventures. After all, in Sweetwater Springs, you never knew what might happen next.

Crumbs of gingerbread lighthouses littered the display case, and the spiced aroma had faded to a murmur of cinnamon and nutmeg. She twirled the delicate silver bracelet around her wrist, a comforting weight against her skin as she recalled Victor's impromptu Christmas Eve surprise.

The bell above the door chimed, breaking the silence of her thoughts.

Gus barreled through the entrance; his eyes bright beneath bushy brows. "Emma! I need your help," he blurted, his words tumbling out in their haste.

She paused, giving him her full attention. "Take a breath. What's got you so worked up?"

He glanced over his shoulder and edged closer. "I'm asking Delilah to marry me."

Emma's lips parted in a slow, dawning grin of delight. "Oh, Gus! That's incredible news. But—how can I help?"

His eyes darted to the display case, then to her. "Those gingerbread houses you make? I was thinking ... could you craft a tiny one, just big enough to hide the ring inside? With a little icing mistletoe on top?"

As Emma listened to Gus's elaborate plan, she grinned. Here was a man utterly undone by love.

"When are you planning on proposing?" she asked.

He gulped. "Tonight."

Her mind spun with ideas. "Perfect. I've got an idea, a gingerbread house with a removable roof to reveal the ring. Festive and romantic enough?"

He pushed out a breath. "You're a genius," he said.

"Thanks. We'll make this happen." She tied her apron securely around her waist and reached for her phone. "I'll call Victor for extra reinforcements."

Within the hour, Victor arrived, bringing with him a flurry of cold air and enthusiasm. "Alright, what's the plan?" he asked, rubbing his hands together.

Emma quickly briefed him. "You're on distraction duty. Keep Delilah occupied while I finish the gingerbread house."

"Doing what?"

"Anything to keep her away from here." Emma swiveled to Gus. "You handle the ring."

"I already have it." He patted his pocket and smiled.

Hours later, the trio set out toward Delilah's house. They cut through the town square, where the Christmas tree towered, its lights flickering like a chaotic rainbow against the indigo dusk. Stray scraps of gift wrap skipped along the curb, outrunning them, while the winter-clean air awaited the year's last hurrah.

Emma cradled the gingerbread house on a makeshift cardboard stretcher, her mittened hands holding one end while Victor gripped the other. They wove through the quiet streets, their careful steps a stark departure from Gus's restless pacing.

"Steady now," Emma instructed as they navigated a patch of ice. "This little house is carrying precious cargo."

Gus's fingers twitched toward his jacket pocket for the umpteenth time, evidently checking for the ring.

"The ring is in the gingerbread house," she reminded him.

"Oh, right." He cast a wary glance at the delicate icing roof. "We should've gone with something less breakable. What if Snowflake knocks it over? That kitten is a terror."

"She looks so sweet," Victor said.

"Looks are deceiving. Believe me, she's not."

Emma chuckled. "Relax, guys. I've cat-proofed the gingerbread house with a dash of citrus. Cats can't stand that smell."

"Clever as always." Victor smiled. "Now if we can get past Mrs. Henderson's yappy dog without a distraction …"

Emma quirked an eyebrow. "Speaking of distractions, how did you manage to keep Delilah occupied today?"

He grinned. "I used my standard Christmas miracle."

"Which is?"

"I told her I needed an emergency consultation on how to remove eggnog stains from an heirloom tablecloth at the Sweetwater Inn, because the owners were upset. A guest had spilled eggnog on it."

"Who?"

"Me, maybe."

"Maybe?"

"Okay, yes it was me. I felt responsible."

"Uh, huh. Go on."

"When I got to Delilah's, I may have accidentally on-purpose tangled us both in a string of lights she had left in her living room, while I reenacted how the 'incident' occurred." He chuckled. "She was laughing too hard to suspect a thing."

Gus's nervous energy gave way to a snort of amusement. "You didn't."

"Oh, I did," Victor confirmed. "I make a convincing damsel in distress when wrapped in Christmas lights."

As they approached Delilah's home, their laughter faded into anticipatory silence. Gus patted his pocket again for the imaginary ring before his gaze flew to the gingerbread house.

A white flash darted across the front window. Snowflake's pale paws soon appeared on the sill. Her blue eyes fixated on the approaching trio, and she let out a high-pitched mew.

"She's onto us," Gus whispered, as if the kitten might somehow overhear their plans.

Emma stifled a laugh. "It's a kitten, Gus, not a security system."

Victor grinned, carefully handing his end of the cardboard to Gus. "I guess that's my cue. Time to put on the performance of a lifetime." He strode ahead to knock on the door, while Gus and Emma tucked themselves behind the bushes.

When Delilah answered, Victor spun a tale about needing help with Christmas returns.

"At this hour?" she asked. "Where are they?"

"I left my car around the corner," he said, maintaining a straight face. "Follow me."

"Wait a minute. Let me grab my coat."

"We'll only be outside for—"

"Hang on. I need my scarf and my boots."

As Victor led Delilah away, Emma and Gus snuck inside. Emma set the gingerbread house on the coffee table while Gus paced back and forth.

"What if she says no?" he muttered.

Emma placed a supportive hand on his arm. "Gus Stratton, that woman has been waiting for you to ask her since high school. Need I remind you she once was our town's matchmaker? She will not say no."

Five minutes later, Delilah's laughter rang out, a sure sign that Victor had performed his job flawlessly.

"You forgot you didn't bring your car?" Delilah asked him.

"I'm scatter-brained recently," he replied.

The door burst open, and Delilah swept in, a whirlwind of color against the winter backdrop. She sported a vibrant peacock-blue coat, its collar studded with costume jewels. Her freshly dyed flame-red hair clashed gloriously with the hot-pink scarf wound haphazardly around her neck. Her feet were encased in leopard-print wellington boots.

"Gus? Emma?" She paused, one hand fixed on the door-knob. A small furrow appeared between her brows. "What's this all about?"

Gus's wavy silver hair caught the light as he grabbed Delilah's hands. The laugh lines around his ocean-blue eyes crinkled. "Delilah Fitzwater," he began, his voice quavering, "you've been a ray of sunshine in my life for longer than I care to admit. It took me years to appreciate what was right in front of me, and I'm done wasting time.'

He lifted the roof of the gingerbread house, revealing the modest diamond ring. Neither large nor flashy, Gus had explained to Emma that it had once belonged to his grandmother.

Kneeling, he gazed up at Delilah. "Will you marry me? Will you make me the happiest man in Sweetwater Springs?"

Delilah's hand flew to her mouth. She sank down, and, for once in her life, she was speechless. She nodded, tears spilling down her cheeks, and yanked Gus to his feet, sealing her answer with a kiss so passionate that Emma and Victor looked away.

"Oh Gus, I'm about to swoon," Delilah gushed. "My dearest sweet potato. I thought you'd never ask."

Emma noiselessly repositioned herself beside Victor, both grinning like teenagers caught in the delightful moment. Snowflake skipped by their feet, adding approving purrs.

As the newly engaged couple celebrated with more kissing, Victor draped his arm around Emma's shoulders. "You really are quite the matchmaker, aren't you, Raindrop?"

She playfully elbowed him in the ribs. "I'm doing my part to keep Sweetwater Springs interesting. Besides, it'll give the gossips something to talk about for weeks."

Their banter was silenced by a muffled thud and the clang of metal on pavement. Delilah, her cheeks still flushed with happiness, froze mid-embrace with Gus. "What was that?"

Emma hurried to the window, pressing her palm to the cold glass. Outside, a figure in a dark coat slinked past an overturned trash can, clutching a canvas tote bag emblazoned with the Sweetwater Springs Historical Society logo.

Gus joined her. "That's odd. The society is closed until after New Year's."

Victor was already halfway to the door. He shouted over his shoulder to Gus and Delilah, "You two stay put. Emma and I will investigate."

Emma quickly buttoned her coat, the frigid air biting at her as she rushed outside. Retreating footsteps sounded as they rounded the corner.

"Hey!" Victor hollered, breaking into a run.

Emma stuck close, her boots pounding against the sidewalk. The figure ahead—a man, judging by his frame—was quick, but she knew these streets like the back of her hand.

They veered into an alley, emerging in time to see the figure turn onto Main Street. With a surge of speed, Victor tackled the man into a wet snowbank, sending them both sprawling. The canvas bag flew open, scattering stacks of cash and checks across the ground.

Her breath faltered as she recognized the person beneath Victor. "James? James McAllister?"

James struggled weakly against Victor's grip. Desperation twisted his features, leaving deep lines across his brow.

"The debts," he panted. "They were going to take everything."

"Who's they?" Emma asked, her voice sharp.

"The bank."

Victor pinned James's arms. His jaw tensed, betraying his simmering anger. "We've found more than a petty thief. Where did all this money come from?"

"I took it from the historical society's fundraiser last week," James muttered, his shoulders hunching as if to ward off their stares. He licked his chapped lips, gaze fixed on a point somewhere between Emma's boots and the scattered cash. "I planned to pay it back before anyone noticed, I swear."

Victor's grip tightened, his wind-burned cheeks taut. "You had access to the funds and used it to cover your debts?"

James nodded, his face pale, as Victor let go of his hands.

Both men stood.

"I've been volunteering there, helping organize the archives. Gus Stratton trusted me ... even gave me the combination to the safe. Said that the McAllister's were good people, and I was a McAllister." James's voice waned. "The money was sitting there. I thought ... I thought I could borrow it for a bit. Save my shop."

Emma's heart twisted. His reasoning seemed all too believable, though it painted an unsettling picture. What had begun as a quiet, uneventful day after Christmas had become far more complicated.

As she phoned the sheriff's office, several shocked neighbors gathered, bundled in winter coats and scarves. Others still wore the cheerful sweaters from yesterday's celebrations. News traveled fast in a small town.

"The fundraiser money." Gus's voice broke through the murmurs, his face ashen. "I left it in the office."

The historical society's annual fundraiser had been a bright spot in the town's Christmas celebrations only a week ago. As treasurer, Gus had mentioned he'd hold off depositing the cash until the holidays had passed. Now, that choice apparently sat like a rock in his gut.

James had access to the office, and the combination to the safe. Was this tied to the rumors of embezzlement that had been plaguing the town for months, or even years?

Delilah appeared, her earlier radiance dimmed by the harsh reality. "Oh, Gus. The McAllisters ... they've been fixtures here since we were born. What could've driven James to this?" Her gaze remained on the cash strewn across the sidewalk, each bill a painful reminder of shattered trust.

Gus stood motionless. The color had drained from his face, leaving him looking almost ghostly in the winter light. "Desperation, I suppose. Money ... it can twist people in ways you wouldn't expect." He exhaled slowly. "I should've been more careful. I should've deposited it before the holiday. I assumed in this town—"

"This town," Delilah interrupted, "is like any other. It has its saints and its sinners, its triumphs and its failures. We're all just people, trying our best, and sometimes we fall short."

Sheriff Randall's cruiser rounded the corner, its lights smearing the snow in alternating red and blue.

Emma locked eyes with Victor. In that fleeting moment, a silent understanding passed between them. The day's joy— Gus and Delilah's engagement, their own peaceful Christmas celebration—had been eclipsed by James's actions.

Emma wrapped her arms around herself. The cold suddenly felt sharper, as if it had seeped beneath her skin. This was Sweetwater Springs, a place where everyone knew each other, where trust had long been the cornerstone of their community. This was a town where doors stayed unlocked, and neighbors watched out for each other.

Despite the betrayal that enveloped her, she clung to her belief in the power of resilience. Sweetwater Springs had weathered its share of trials before, and this, too, would pass. The specialness of the residents—their fortitude and character—would endure.

CHAPTER 14

 he interrogation room at the Sweetwater Springs police station appeared smaller than Emma remembered. She sat across from James McAllister, his face a conflicting mix of shame and defiance. Sheriff Randall stood close, his expression as unyielding as stone.

"James confessed," the sheriff stated, his voice firm. "He's been embezzling for a while."

"Why, James?" Emma asked. "Why steal from the town?"

He seemed to fold in on himself—shoulders sagging, as if the heaviness of his admission had finally caught up to him. "*McAllister's Game Haven* was failing," he muttered. "I couldn't watch it go under. Not after everything my parents sacrificed to help me start a business."

As he laid out his story—debts piling higher than his ability to manage, the ensuing panic—Emma understood on some level. She, too, had wrestled with the pressure of living up to family expectations.

"I never meant for it to go this far," he continued. "I couldn't bear to be the failure. Everyone respected my parents, and I thought ... I thought I had to live up to that."

Emma's throat felt thick, as if her emotions were choking her. Her mind flashed back to the nights spent agonizing over *Blissful Bites*, wondering if she'd ever measure up to the dream her parents had built.

James glanced at the sheriff, his gaze flickering nervously, before landing back on Emma. "There's more," he said, his voice dropping to a near whisper. "I'm not the only person involved."

Sheriff Randall stepped forward, eyes narrowing. "What do you mean?"

James's hands fidgeted in his lap. "I saw something. Late one night at the historical society. Mr. Garrison—the antique shop owner—was there. Arguing with someone. They were talking about … moving money, covering up things."

A rush of adrenaline surged through Emma.

Mr. Garrison? The gentle, elderly guy who'd sold her Victor's vintage camera?

"Did you recognize who he was quarrelling with?" Sheriff Randall pressed.

James shook his head. "No, but I heard a name. Thompson."

Emma gasped. Mayor Jim Thompson? The man everyone held in high regard?

The room stuttered for a beat. The implications of what James revealed were chilling.

"James," Emma said. "Why didn't you come forward with this earlier?"

He looked up, guilt darkening his eyes. "I was already in too deep. I assumed if I could fix things at the shop, make enough to pay everything back, it would all go away. Instead, it only got worse."

A flood of empathy surged within her. She was well aware of the sentiment, the desperate optimism that any trouble disappeared if one clung firmly to the past.

"The fear of failure," she murmured. "You're pushed to do things you never imagined."

James nodded quickly, as if her understanding offered him a brief reprieve.

As the sheriff pressed on with more questions, Emma's mind turned. The bombshell about Mr. Garrison and Mayor Thompson brought a disturbing twist to the case. Beyond the unfolding mystery, James's confession hit her in a place she hadn't expected—his struggle was a mirror to her own. Both were smothered by the gravity of expectancies. Both feared disappointing those who mattered most.

Outside the station, Victor waited. As soon as she stepped into the cold, he gathered her into his embrace.

"How are you holding up?" he asked.

Emma rested her head on his chest, and her tension slowly ebbed away. "James revealed more than I expected. And ... I hate to admit it, but I understand him more than I want to." She looked up into Victor's eyes, finding the concern and understanding she sought. "His fear of failing, of letting down his family—is not all that different from mine."

"Emma, you're nothing like him. You haven't done anything wrong."

"I might have, though," she whispered. "If circumstances were different, if I'd been anxious enough ..." She trailed off, absorbing the realization.

Victor lifted her chin. "You didn't. You're facing your fears head-on and moving forward, not backward." His eyes searched hers. "Is that why you've been reluctant to clear out the storage room?"

Emma stiffened, the question hitting closer to home than she expected. The cluttered back room of *Blissful Bites* had been a source of contention between them, with Victor urging her to sort through the years of baking paraphernalia and outdated supplies.

"I've made progress," she said, though her voice quivered. "I find it hard to part with anything."

His arms tightened around her. "Remember what you've accomplished. You're at the heart of this investigation. Knowledge, instincts—you've brought us closer to answers. You're stronger than you give yourself credit for."

His words helped soothe her nagging self-doubts. She was truly seen and appreciated. Even so, beneath the reassurance, a tiny knot of uncertainty refused to fully dissolve.

"I'm afraid of what I might lose if I remove years of possessions from my life." Her confession slipped out before she had the ability to stop herself. She drew away from him abruptly, muttering an excuse about needing to check on muffins she may have left in the oven.

"Emma, you've been away from the bakery for hours. Muffins would've burnt to a crisp by now." His lips parted, as if he had more to say, but the words didn't form. He glanced around, searching for an answer that wasn't there.

She wanted to let him in, to explore their increasing connection, but the fear of getting hurt, of disrupting the tenuous balance she'd managed to create, held her captive.

Victor took her hand, his thumb drawing relaxing circles on her palm. "What if I help you? We'll tackle the project together. We'll keep what matters most."

She found the courage to nod. "Okay." Her voice was fierce enough to seal the promise.

Once they started walking, they were greeted by a commotion in the square. Several parents and children congregated beneath a towering tree, their faces a blend of furrowed brows and wide, expectant eyes.

Before they could investigate further, Sheriff Randall

approached them, his face pale and tired, mirroring the passage of a long day. "Emma, Victor, we've got a problem."

They stepped aside, and the sheriff lowered his voice. "Some folks are having trouble accepting James's confession. They're calling his arrest a cover-up for someone bigger."

Her heart sank. "We have evidence. Mayor Thompson was involved."

"Try telling that to the residents," Sheriff Randall sighed. "There's a gathering outside the town hall. They're demanding we reopen the investigation, claiming we've got the wrong people."

A silent conversation passed between Victor and Emma in the blink of a moment. The truth they'd worked so hard to uncover was being buried under a wave of disbelief and misplaced loyalty.

Emma squared her shoulders. "We can't let this stand."

Victor nodded.

As they discussed how to address this new challenge, a child's shout drew their attention back to the gathering beneath the towering tree.

High above, nestled precariously among the branches, was Snowflake, Delilah's spirited kitten, her white fur glaring against the gnarled bark.

Victor's focus sharpened. With purposeful strides, he approached the tree, shrugging off his coat as if the climb ahead didn't faze him. Determination flashed in his eyes, unwavering as he scanned the branches for the safest path up. "I'll get her," he said, his confidence like a steady flame.

"Victor, wait!" Emma's voice trembled. "Your leg—you've still got that limp."

"I'm fine," he replied, his tone sure.

Without hesitation, he began his climb, every movement deliberate as he worked his way up the tree. He seemed unfazed, his entire being focused on the tiny, cowering kitten. From below, Emma sensed Victor's heartbeat, solid and unwavering.

Snowflake clung to a branch, her body shaking like a leaf trapped in a gust of wind.

"Hey there, little one." Victor extended his hand, palm up, in a calm invitation. "It's safe. I've got you."

Snowflake blinked at him, uncertain.

In one swift, gentle motion, he scooped the kitten into his arms. Once he descended, careful and measured, the gathering erupted into cheers. Victor's face lit with a sincere smile as he handed the kitten to a breathless Delilah, who had rushed forward.

"Oh, thank you!" She clutched the kitten to her chest as if she were holding a precious jewel.

Emma stood back, her heart swelling with affection, while Victor interacted with the children. His kindness radiated, causing all her other thoughts to fade—the tension, the investigation, the uncertainty.

He advanced, brushing off his hands before leaning in for a quick kiss, then grabbing his coat. "I'll call you later, okay?"

She smiled. "Yes, of course."

Unease curled in her stomach as she watched his retreating figure. His dedication and perseverance were qualities she admired, yet a part of her wondered how long they'd last as a couple once the case was wrapped up. People had a way of leaving her behind. She'd learned the hard way that opening up often led to heartache. As much as she wanted to trust him completely, and believe in their relationship, the fear of being left alone held her back.

The day after James's startling confession, Emma and Victor found themselves in the dimly lit basement of the town hall. Sheriff Randall had granted them permission to sift through records in search of anything related to the embezzlement scheme.

Victor lifted a crumbling ledger from a box labeled '1950-1960.'

"These go way back," he said, flipping through the yellowed pages.

Emma peered over his shoulder and scanned the figures and notations. "This is more than bookkeeping. The patterns —subtle shifts, funds being shuffled around. Exactly what we've been currently seeing, although it started decades ago."

They pored over the documents—letters, memos, even personal journals—and a complex story emerged. This was more than a crime. This was a secret that had been passed down through generations of leaders, involving several mayors.

"They believed they were protecting the town," Emma murmured, reading a letter penned by a former mayor. "During the recession in the 50s, they started siphoning off money into a 'rainy day' account. They were afraid the federal government would step in if the town went bankrupt."

Victor nodded grimly. "And it kept going. Each elected mayor was sworn into the secret, told it was for the greater good."

Emma sat back on her heels, her mind reeling. "Mayor Thompson is the latest in a long line. He probably assumes he's doing what's best for Sweetwater Springs."

"Even if the method he employs is totally misguided," Victor added.

This wasn't only one person's mistake. This was woven into the town's history, rooted in good intentions, though riddled with corruption. A legacy passed through generations, both noble and flawed.

. . .

THE NEXT MORNING, Emma and Victor stood at the entrance of Mayor Thompson's office, the late December chill sharp against their skin. Outside, the square lay soundless, with remnants of the holiday garlands still draped over the lamp-posts, their lively reds and greens muted in the colorless winter light. Inside, the town hall only heightened the tension in the air, the cheer oddly out of place, dulled by what had been revealed.

Inside the mayor's office, the room felt tired, as though it had absorbed the strain of secrets long kept. A once-lively poinsettia drooped in the corner, its leaves curling and dry, while the holiday lights that framed the windows blinked sporadically, causing erratic shadows over the cluttered desk. The dim light filtering through the overcast sky outside gave the chamber a somber, melancholic hue.

Mayor Thompson looked up from his desk. His features, faded and lined, had the look of someone who had seen too much.

"Emma, Victor," he greeted, his voice stripped of its usual confidence. "What brings you here?"

"Mayor Thompson, we're aware of the embezzlement." Victor wasted no time in speaking. "We know it's been happening for decades."

"Ridiculous accusation. Where's your proof?"

"Here." Victor placed the documents on the mayor's desk. "Right here."

The mayor scarcely glanced at the documents. Instead, he blew out a long breath. "I tried to protect what was built," he murmured, his voice scarcely a thread. "The world is changing so fast, but Sweetwater Springs … is different. I didn't want to see it fall apart. Not on my watch."

"At what cost?" Emma asked. "The trust of the very people who looked up to you for guidance?"

As the truth unknotted, Emma, emotions colliding

between empathy and betrayal. This wasn't only the mayor's secret to bear—this was a legacy they all were forced to confront.

In the days following the revelation, Sweetwater Springs was a place of turmoil. Emergency meetings were held, audits were conducted, and difficult conversations took place in every home and business.

Mayor Thompson resigned, apparently bracing himself for the legal fallout of his choices. Yet, as the initial shock wore off, a remarkable story unfolded. The town didn't crumble under the burden of the scandal. Instead, Sweetwater Springs rallied. Residents connected with each other, and local businesses united. What might have torn them apart instead brought them closer.

One evening, Victor spread out several documents on the table in the back storage room. "Here's what we've pieced together," he summarized to Emma. "For decades, town officials pocketed insignificant amounts from various funds—the holiday market, renovation projects, even the school budget. They created fake invoices and inflated costs."

Emma frowned. "A sizable amount of money?"

"Yes. Some of it went into a secret 'rainy day' account that, as you know, was claimed was for emergencies. However, a significant portion was distributed among the conspirators. Mayor Thompson and Mr. Garrison were the main beneficiaries in recent years."

"No one noticed?" she asked.

"Nope. It was death by a thousand cuts for the town's finances. Mr. Garrison has also been arrested, and his business is shuttered."

At a town hall meeting the following afternoon, Gus Stratton sprang to his feet. "Folks, what happened was wrong. Nonetheless, Sweetwater Springs is more than the mistakes of a few. We're a community and have always taken care of our own. That's who we are, and it's non-negotiable."

Nods of agreement rippled through the room. Even those who had initially resisted the truth nodded in acceptance.

Emma's shoulders relaxed. The town was finally ready to face reality and move forward.

James McAllister, tackling the immensity of his mistakes, offered to help in any way he could.

Emma and Victor left the meeting, hand in hand, and spotted Mayor Thompson. He stood alone at the edge of the square, silhouetted by the fading light of day. For a second, they hesitated, but then, as if tugged by a shared instinct, they approached him.

"I'm sorry," the former mayor whispered. "I never intended for things to spiral so far out of control."

Emma rested her hand on his arm. "What you did was wrong, but now you have the chance to make amends."

Victor gave a measured nod. "Sweetwater Springs is resilient. Tougher than any secret or misstep."

They turned to walk away, and a delicate thread of hope wound its way through Emma's chest. The town had been shaken to its very core, its lies unearthed, though the ties that bound the people remained steadfast.

She glanced at Victor, seeing the same unspoken thought in his eyes. They had uncovered rawness and pain. In doing so, they had offered Sweetwater Springs a chance to rebuild —sounder, wiser, and with roots deeper than ever before.

CHAPTER 15

*L*ater that day, the townsfolk grappled with the aftermath of confessions while Emma and Victor tackled the storage room. The task was Herculean, filled with laughter, tears, and rediscovered treasures.

Emma's hands shook as she picked up a mixing bowl, its ceramic surface chipped and washed out.

"This was Mom's favorite," she murmured, her voice catching.

Victor took the bowl from her. "We can keep it if you want."

Emma shook her head, then nodded, then shook it again. "I … I can't …"

Her breath came in short gasps. "This is too much," she choked out, sinking to the floor.

He knelt beside her, his hand warm on her back. "Hey, it's fine. We can take a break."

"No, you don't understand. Every item here is a piece of my family. Of me. Once it's gone, what's left?" She clutched a bundle of recipe cards, their dog-eared corners poking between her fingers.

He lifted her chin. "Emma, you're more than these things. Your parents, your remembrances—they're in here." He tapped his chest. "Not in bowls for mixing or cards with recipes."

Her tears fell freely. "What if I forget? What if I lose them all over again?"

"You won't," he promised. "Because you'll continue to create lasting memories. You'll use those recipes and share stories about that mixing bowl. Their essence will endure through you, not through these objects."

She took a shuddering breath, examining the disorderly room. What lay before her resembled a confinement rather than a refuge, the walls closing in as a result of her own choices.

"Okay," she whispered. "Let's continue." She stood and wiped her eyes. With unsteady hands, she placed the mixing bowl in the donate pile. It wasn't easy, but it was a start.

Emma shared stories—the significance of her grand-mother's cherished rolling pin, the importance of a chipped mug from her first baking competition. Victor listened attentively, asking questions and offering tender encourage-ment when Emma's resolve wavered.

As the room slowly transformed, so did Emma. With each item she relinquished, the chains of yesterday lifted off her shoulders. The space began to breathe, and so did she.

"Victor," she said, placing another box of items by the door, "I finally understand why this embezzlement case was so hard to crack."

"Why?"

"I've held onto things for ages, burying important stuff under layers of junk. The town's finances were the same way. Years of suppression and camouflage, until the truth was so concealed nobody could find it."

"True," he agreed. "We looked for a single big discrepancy,

although sometimes it's buried under many tiny ones instead."

The same evening, they sat amidst boxes of sorted items, and Victor picked up a faded black-and-white photograph. "Who's this?" he asked, showing Emma the image of a young woman standing proudly in front of a shiny new oven.

Emma beamed, a bittersweet ache in her chest. "My mom, on the day she opened the bakery." She outlined the woman's face with a gentle finger. "I've always been afraid of not living up to the impact she made. I guess that's why I held onto so much stuff—I could keep her close that way."

He wrapped an arm around her shoulders. "You honor her every day. Not by clinging to the past, but by building on the foundation she laid. By making *Blissful Bites* your own."

As his message sank in, she surveyed the half-cleared room, seeing it not as a repository of memories, but as a space full of possibilities.

"You're right," she said.

Despite her words, she hesitated. Her gaze fell on an old cash register, a relic from her parents' time. Her friends had suggested she invest in a modern point-of-sale system, although the idea of parting with this piece of her past sent a pang through her chest. Instead, after Victor left, she spent the subsequent hour polishing the register, convincing herself that its vintage charm was part of *Blissful Bites'* appeal.

The familiar beckons, even when unwelcome, she mused, lightly wiping down the brass keys. She was making progress. But the register—well, that would take more time.

THE MORNING AFTER, Emma stood in front of *Blissful Bites*, a CLOSED FOR RENOVATIONS sign in her hand. She hung the sign on the door, then stood motionless.

Victor appeared at her side, a supportive touch on her back. "Ready for more of this?" he asked.

She tilted her chin in a decisive motion. "Ready. After the Christmas rush, business usually slows down as we head into January."

Taking a deep breath, she thought back to the call she had made to request the loan. Mr. Granger, the bank manager, had hesitated at first, wary of lending to someone struggling to make ends meet. However, he had known her parents well.

Emma had poured her heart into the conversation, sharing her vision for *Blissful Bites,* her love for the bakery, and how renovations could transform it into an even more welcoming haven for the community. After a lengthy discussion, they agreed to a modest loan—enough to cover her vision and the renovations.

She remembered the conversation she'd had with Victor hours before her phone call.

"If you need the money, I'd be happy to help," he had offered, his tone earnest. She had appreciated the gesture, but a flicker of resistance had risen within her.

No, she needed to prove to herself that she could build her dream independently, even if it meant taking a risk. The bakery was her heart and soul, and she wanted to ensure its success on her own terms.

She turned to find James McAllister sweeping the sidewalk. His shoulders drooped as if an unseen force anchored him to the ground.

"James?" Emma called, surprise coloring her voice.

He raised his gaze, offering a tentative smile. "Morning, Emma. I, uh, thought I'd lend a hand around town. Not much, but …"

She nodded. "It's a start."

The next day, she stepped inside the bakery and studied

her reflection in the window. The woman staring back at her looked different—lighter, more confident. In letting go of the physical clutter, she was also releasing her own emotional baggage.

Down the street, James McAllister neared the historical society, his back to her as he lugged in chairs for an upcoming meeting. Apparently, he had begun the community service project he'd been assigned as part of his restitution.

His head was bowed, his broad shoulders bearing a burden that went beyond physical exhaustion. Nonetheless, even at a distance, she recognized the flicker of determination in his eyes.

"James," she called out. "How are you holding up?"

He stilled, then turned, a tired smile forming at the corners of his mouth. "I'm facing each day as it comes, I suppose. This community service is eye-opening. I never fully understood the scale of effort to keep this place running —the extent of what I took for granted."

Emma crossed the street and smiled an acknowledgement. "You're making a difference," she said.

He massaged his temples. "*The Game Haven* is gone for good. However, I've been thinking." For a heartbeat, he looked vulnerable, as though unsure of how she'd receive what came next. "Maybe I could use my knowledge of tactics and do something right for once. I've talked to the school, trying to get a strategy club started for the high schoolers."

"James, how—" Her next breath lodged somewhere between lung and lips. "How wonderful."

His smile grew. "Only a start," he said, meeting her eyes with a rare honesty. "I've got a long way to go. But I'm trying. That's all I can do."

"Trying is enough for now."

A lone gull cried overhead, disappearing into the background, leaving only a shared acknowledgement of past mistakes, and the tentative expectation of something better ahead.

James McAllister became a fixture in Sweetwater Springs' recovery efforts. He organized a town cleanup, rallying volunteers to spruce up the park. At the center, he tutored kids struggling with math, his game shop skills finding a renewed purpose.

Emma overheard Mrs. Chen at the market. "That James McAllister, he's really made a fresh start. Helped me carry my groceries yesterday, wouldn't take no for an answer."

Sweetwater Springs was evolving. And so was Emma. As she walked back to the bakery, Victor met her at the entrance and smiled a greeting.

Whatever challenges lay ahead, she'd face them—soaring above previous hardships and buoyed by the promise of the future.

The renovation was only the beginning. The best chapter of her life was yet to be written.

ANOTHER DAY PASSED, and Emma measured the progress in her half-finished bakery space, paintbrush in hand. The walls, once jumbled with outdated decor, stood bare, waiting for a fresh coat of paint. The countertops had been torn out, making way for sleek surfaces that would house her latest creations.

The air was thick with the scent of plaster and sawdust. In one corner, a pair of electricians debated the placement of light fixtures, their voices competing with the rhythmic scrape of a sander nearby.

She dabbed at a paint swatch on the newly smoothed

wall, considering a terracotta hue. The gutted interior, stripped of its dated charm, hummed with potential. Where antique display cases once stood, chalk outlines on the concrete floor mapped out sleek, modern counters.

The hollow sound of footsteps on the plywood pathway heralded a makeshift bell—a string of jingle bells hung on the plastic sheeting that served as a temporary door. James McAllister ducked under a sheet of plastic, his gaze bouncing from the exposed beams to the drop cloth-covered floors.

"Emma," he said. "Can we talk?"

"Of course." She set her brush in a water-filled mason jar. "Mind the wet paint."

He navigated the obstacle path of tools and materials and smiled. "The place is really shaping up."

"Thanks. How are you?"

"Every hour is challenging." His smile faded. "I'm at a loss in many respects, to be honest."

She nudged a piece of shelving that had fallen on the floor with her foot. "Any progress on your strategy club idea for the school?"

"The administration is discussing offering a course for the high schoolers. Nothing concrete yet."

"Actually," she swiveled to face him. "I have another idea."

Over the next hour, Emma outlined her plans for expanding *Blissful Bites*, not only as a bakery but as a community space. She spoke of game nights, of blending James's passion for games with her baking expertise to create a unique gathering place. This was growth. This was healing. This was what Sweetwater Springs was about—creating a supportive environment, solidarity, and the power of coming together.

After he left, the bells jingled again, and Victor strode in. "Was that James I saw leaving?" he asked, checking over his shoulder.

She nodded, wiping her hands on her paint-splattered overalls. "I offered him a job—providing game nights here. It'll be good for him. For everyone."

"Tonight is New Year's Eve. Can I treat you to dinner?"

"I can't. I hope to open the bakery back up in another week, and there's too much to do. In all honesty, I'm all holi-dayed out anyway."

"Is that a word?" he asked.

She grinned. "Anyway?"

"Holidayed."

"It is now."

He returned her grin. "A raincheck in January, then? Deal?"

"Sure. Deal."

He crossed the space and pressed a brief, heartfelt kiss to her lips. "You're remarkable, Emma Jacobsen. Always bringing peace where it's needed most."

Her cheeks flushed at his compliment.

"Thank you," she replied as she stepped away.

It should've been comforting, these sweet exchanges between them. Instead, it left her anxious, as if everything was moving too smoothly, too perfectly.

His hand found the edge of the plywood counter, his fingers grazing hers. "You're bringing restoration to this town."

A sudden clatter from the back room broke the moment —someone had knocked over a toolbox. Emma started, nearly upsetting a can of primer on the floor.

"I better get back to work," she said, gesturing vaguely at the half-painted wall. "These renovations won't finish themselves."

"Need an extra pair of hands? I'm handy with a paint-brush, even on New Year's Eve."

She glanced at her watch. "It's not New Year's Eve until this evening."

"Same difference."

"Okay, then. I can use all the help I can get. There are two walls left to be painted." She handed him a roller. "Don't entertain any ideas about redecorating, though. I've got a vision for this place."

Although they worked side by side, the easy rhythm of the painting didn't quell her disquiet. His growing closeness triggered her deep-seated fears of vulnerability and loss, causing her to instinctively withdraw from the emotional intimacy he represented.

"I should check the new convection ovens," she blurted. "They were delivered earlier, and I want to make sure they don't have any dents." She gestured vaguely toward the back room.

"What? Why now? Emma, what's wrong?"

"Nothing." She cut him off. "I'm fine. Things are crazy busy and I'm distracted."

He opened his mouth to respond, though she was already retreating to where her ovens would be placed, her future sanctuary.

"Happy New Year," he called to her an hour later. "The walls are finished, and I'll text you tonight."

"Okay," she called back.

The jingle of bells signaled his departure.

Alone, she braced herself against the cool metal of a prep table, willing her heart to slow. She was being ridiculous. Victor had given her no reason to doubt him. Yet, a voice in her head kept broadcasting words like abandonment and loss, growing louder with each passing hour.

Outside, twilight was falling.

Emma steeled her spine, forcing down the tumult of

emotions. She had a bakery to renovate, a town to help heal. She didn't have time to fret about worries that weren't even there.

Little did she know that in mere hours, her carefully constructed world would come crashing down around her.

CHAPTER 16

*N*ew Year's Day. A public holiday. But Emma was too busy to notice.

Late morning slouched over the Pacific Northwest, the sun a mere smudge behind gauze-thick clouds. She flipped the CLOSED FOR RENOVATION sign on the door of *Blissful Bites* and sighed. Fatigue pressed in, a result of the early start and hours spent painting the previous day.

Her ensemble spoke of work: a plum-hued down jacket, its cuffs flecked with remnants of paint chips, over jeans, a long-sleeved shirt, and sturdy clogs. A powdery smell of paint clung to her hair, tucked haphazardly under a cable-knit beanie pulled low over her ears.

The town square sat quiet, but for the occasional clink of shopkeepers opening their doors, preparing for New Year's Day sales. Christmas had been over days ago, leaving the square adrift in the doldrums after the holidays. A half-deflated balloon, somehow missed in the post-celebration cleanup, bobbed forlornly against a tree stump.

Victor had asked to meet for an early lunch, and she smiled at the thought of seeing him. He was the one. He completed the empty spaces inside herself that she'd tried hard to suppress. Yet there was a distance about him, a part of him that eluded her grasp.

She wrapped her arms around herself as she crossed the square and walked toward a bench by an oak tree. It had become their place when he'd first come to town, a silent witness to conversations that had left her both hopeful and vulnerable.

Today had a distinct sensation, though. Not only because it was New Year's Day—new beginning and all that. It was as if a monumental decision was waiting to be made.

Victor was already there, leaning against the tree with a calm confidence that never wavered. His tailored wool topcoat, in a rich espresso hue, repelled the persistent drizzle with quiet efficiency. A cashmere scarf in a heathered slate blue lay folded at his collar, its herringbone pattern a nod to practicality without sacrificing style. Typical Victor. Always sophisticated.

He offered her a smile, one that failed to chase away the shadows lurking in her mind.

"Hey," he said, taking a step toward her. "Happy New Year."

"Happy New Year," she replied, trying to match his pleasant tone.

"You didn't respond to my texts last night."

"Sorry," she said. "I was exhausted and couldn't stay awake until midnight. I fell asleep by ten."

Before she had the chance to say more, he cupped her chin and pressed his lips to hers in a tender kiss. For a heartbeat, certainty blurred at the edges, but as they parted, her disquiet crept back, refusing to loosen its grip.

Her eyes mapped his handsome face, each glance etching his features deeper into her memory. Why this sense of foreboding? She didn't want to over analyze it. Not today.

"I've been thinking," he said, his voice low.

"Oh? About what?" She waited for him to continue, her fingers trailing the outline of a stray cookie cutter in her tote bag.

His phone vibrated in his coat pocket. He hesitated, glancing at the screen, then back at her. "I should—"

"Go ahead," she said, forcing a smile. "It's fine."

He stepped away to take the call, his tone hushed like a librarian's whisper, though a chill settled over her heart. She tried to ignore the feeling, assuring herself that the caller was Elliot or Gus, and had nothing to do with her. Nonetheless, the nagging sense of a loss wouldn't be quieted.

Minutes passed and Victor's conversation dragged on. His expression shifted from focused to unreadable. Finally, he clicked off and turned to her. A muscle twitched in his cheek. For a heartbeat, he studied the cracks in the sidewalk, then his eyes locked on hers, steady yet shadowed.

"Emma, something has come up."

"What is it?" she asked, though her heart was already bracing for the answer she didn't want to hear.

"That was the Bureau. There's been a breakthrough in a case. They are interested in hiring me immediately and need me in D.C. tomorrow."

"So sudden? It's a holiday." The words slipped out, the disbelief thick in her voice. "Aren't all government offices closed?

"Today is a holiday. Not tomorrow. However, essential services and law enforcement duties continue as needed, so there is staff on call for critical operations." He hesitated. "To be fair, they first contacted me several days ago."

"You didn't mention anything."

"I should have, but you're dealing with so much—the renovations …" He trailed off.

"What does that mean? Are you going? Just like that?

What about your New Year's raincheck to take me out to dinner?"

"I haven't forgotten. Besides, I thought you were holidayed out." His gaze rested on her, patient, yet probing.

That was yesterday, she wanted to say. Instead, she said nothing.

"I'll make it up to you." He closed the gap separating them with measured steps. "This is my dream job, Emma."

His declaration landed with the force of a gavel, each syllable chipping away at the foundations of their shared future. Somehow, she had an intuition that this moment would arrive; she had sensed it in the background ever since he had reemerged in her life.

"Right," she said quietly, as she tried to hold herself together. "Your job."

"Growing up, my parents never stayed in one place long enough for me to experience a sense of belonging. The FBI is a chance to be part of something bigger while making a difference," he continued. "This position is about protecting people, about providing the stability I wish I had. I can help prevent the type of crimes that uproot families and that force kids to grow up always looking over their shoulder."

"What about the roots you've put down here? What we've built?"

"This ... this is something I must do. Long-distance relationships are common. We can work it out."

A bitter laugh escaped her, harsh and unbidden. "How can you say that, Victor? You're walking away. Again." Her tone cracked, and she blinked back tears she refused to let fall. "I thought this time was different between us."

"It is. I love you, Emma. This is an opportunity I've wanted all my adult life. I can't refuse."

"What am I supposed to do while you're off saving the country?' Her voice shook, the emotions too raw, too tangled to keep inside. "Wait around? Pretend like it doesn't hurt each time you leave?"

"I'll fly back here on holidays. Whenever you want, you can fly to D.C." Victor kneaded the back of his neck, his expression cycling through a silent film of emotions. "This isn't the end of us."

Or was it?

Every fear she'd kept buried was coming true.

"The truth is, you're leaving, Victor," she breathed. "Maybe that's who you are."

He extended his hand. Refusing, Emma took a half-step back, her coat rustling. The inch of air separating his fingers from her sleeves might as well have been a chasm.

"Emma. Please. Don't overcomplicate this more than it already is. Let's make a plan."

"For a long-distance relationship?" She lifted her chin. "I can't. Not again. I won't wait around, hoping you'll return."

His face remained inscrutable, a mask she could no longer decipher with certainty. The silence was strained, elastic, and brittle. She could see the conflict in his eyes—the war between his emotions and his duty. It didn't matter. She already knew how it would end.

She swiveled and marched away, her steps slow but certain, her heart breaking. The wind whipped through the square, cold and biting, although she was scarcely aware of it. An ache settled deep in her chest. The realization that she'd been foolish to believe their relationship could've been different this time.

Behind her, the town clock chimed twelve times, each peal reminding her of what might have been. The sound reverberated through the square, marking noon and the end of a chapter she hadn't been ready to close.

. . .

VICTOR REMAINED MOTIONLESS, caught between two worlds —the familiar thrill of the chase calling from D.C., and the unexpected love he'd found in this small town. As Emma's silhouette faded into the early afternoon, he wondered if he'd made the biggest mistake of his life.

THE DAYS after Victor's departure passed in a muted blur. A fine mist hung over Sweetwater Springs, the moisture clinging to every surface. The streets glistened under the dim winter light, reflecting holiday decorations not yet taken down. Patches of old snow, more gray than white, clung doggedly to darkened corners, a reminder of the month's rare snowfalls.

Emma went through the motions and reopened *Blissful Bites*.

The renovations were complete, and she busied herself by preparing orders for comfort foods—cinnamon rolls and sourdough bread, though her heart wasn't in it. She replayed Victor's final words, the phrase looping in her mind like a skipping record.

She hadn't responded to his constant texts. Each chime of her phone stirred a cluster of emotions—hope, sadness, a flicker of anger. What options did she have for a response? There were no words to loosen the knot forming beneath her ribs.

She decided to offer health-conscious baked goods for people looking for healthier options because of their New Year's resolutions and advertised in the local newspaper.

Immersing herself in her work, she tried to numb the endless sadness in her gut. But the pain was always there, settling in with the same permanence as the misty rain outside.

Victor had promised her that his job wouldn't change

anything, that leaving for D.C. was merely another part of his life. But it had changed everything. She felt it in the way the silence lingered in her apartment, in the way her hands stilled as she prepared her recipes, in the way her heart kept time with a leaden rhythm.

As the town braced for the winter months ahead—overcast skies and steady rainfall—families and friends congregated in the square, their animated chatter and jovial smiles a sharp divide between them and her solitude. She wondered if this was how her life would be again—watching the people she loved slip away while she remained behind.

Each evening, she'd study her phone, her heart twisting at the texts from Victor, before setting it aside. His messages had come in waves, one after another, each unread notification reminding her of the distance growing between them.

What could she possibly say? Anything she managed would only sound bitter, and bitterness wasn't her. Or at least, she didn't want it to be. Though, seeing the world move in pairs, celebrating the new year, the agony of solitude gnawed deeper.

THE WASHINGTON MONUMENT pierced the sky like a needle through fabric, its simple white surface a clear distinction from the pulsing metropolis below. Victor stood at the window of his hotel room, his reflection pale in the glass. The FBI badge he'd dreamed of for years lay untouched on the nightstand; its shine was duller than he'd imagined. He studied it, though the thrill he expected didn't come. Instead, memories of Sweetwater Springs ambushed him—the jingle of Emma's bakery bell, her flour-dusted apron, and the smile that lit up her face when she greeted customers.

He texted her again. Once again, it remained unanswered.

A tightness coiled in his stomach, twisting firmer with each breath. He could almost smell the cinnamon and butter that invariably clung to her hair, almost hear the chatter of regulars swapping gossip over steaming mugs of coffee and piping hot cinnamon rolls. Sweetwater Springs had attached to him like sap on a pine tree, its spirit soaking into every corner of his being.

His shoes clicked against the polished hardwood floor as he paced. The glass coffee table reflected the city lights, its surface unmarked by coasters or family photos. On the wall, a modern geometric painting stared back at him, all sharp angles and muted colors. No scent of freshly baked bread, no mismatched mugs, no messy but cherished recipe collections. Only clean lines and empty spaces.

"Get it together, Steele," he muttered. "This is what you've always wanted."

Was it? The thought hit him like a sucker punch. He'd pursued this goal with tunnel vision, never considering if the finish line still held the prize he once envisioned.

Emma's face flashed in his mind—her blue eyes sparkling as she laughed, flour dusting her cheek. The way she'd looked at him that last day, hurt and betrayal etched across her features.

His lungs went cold. He'd made a terrible mistake.

He grabbed his phone, fingers flying over the keys as he booked the earliest flight out back to the state of Washington. Then he'd rent a car to drive to Sweetwater Springs. His heart beat double time, though for the first time since he'd arrived in D.C., he regained the ability to breathe.

"Hang on, Emma," he whispered. "I'm coming home."

By the tenth day after Victor had left, Emma stood by the shop window, her breath misting the glass. The cold seeped into her bones, deeper than it ever had before, until the beauty of the town could no longer reach her.

She turned away, surveying her empty bakery in the dim afternoon light.

She'd completed all the renovations. The creamy white paint on the walls brightened the appearance, and she had updated the floors to durable reclaimed wood. The seating had gotten a retro makeover, with tables and chairs featuring touches of metal accents and bright yellow cushions.

She'd decided on vintage-inspired pendant lights, which gave the area a cozy glow.

She modernized the display cases with glass-front counters to showcase her baked goods—pies, cakes, cookies, and breads—while maintaining a handmade touch. Butcher block counters gave a clean, polished look, and she stocked shelves behind the counter with bags of coffee and homemade jams.

However, this evening, the display cases, usually brimming with cinnamon-spiced star cookies and snickerdoodle cookies, stood bare.

She hadn't had the heart to bake anything beyond the day's basic needs. With a sigh, she reached for a broom, determined to at least keep her hands busy.

Her mind wandered to Victor. By now, he had started his exciting career in D.C. She paused, leaning on the broom handle, allowing herself one flicker of weakness to imagine what might have been.

The jingle of the bell above the door startled her. She looked up, ready to inform the latecomer that the shop was closed. As usual, she'd forgotten to lock the door.

The stillness shattered as a male voice called out. "Emma!"

She whirled around; the broom clattering to the floor. There, framed in the doorway, stood Victor—his presence as unexpected as summer snow.

His face was flushed, his breaths ragged as if he'd been running. A fine mist clung to his wool coat.

"Victor? What are you doing here? I thought you were—" She stopped herself, unsure of what to say.

His lips quirked upward, a tentative grin breaking across his features. "D.C. can keep its job," he murmured, each step toward her deliberate. His gaze never left hers, as if he feared she might vanish if he blinked. "I'm staying here, Emma. Right here in Sweetwater Springs."

Her heart leapt at his words, although caution—born from an entrenched fear—restrained her.

"What about your job?" she asked. "Your dream?"

His hands found hers, the warmth of him radiating through her fingers.

"I've realized something," he said, voice muted, as if he were confessing a guarded secret. "My dream isn't a job, or some city far away. My dream, Emma, is here. It's you. This town, this life. The life we can build together."

Her breath faltered. The bakery narrowing to just the two of them.

"Our ... life?" The words stumbled out.

"Yes. I don't want the job," he repeated, his conviction unmistakable. "I want you, Emma. If you'll have me."

Her heart thundered in her chest, her thoughts trying to catch up with reality.

"Emma Jacobsen." He fumbled in his pocket before holding up a dazzling diamond engagement ring, expertly cut into a glittering round shape, its flawless stone shimmering in the light. "Will you marry me?" He spoke each syllable with measured precision.

Her breaths narrowed to the single heartbeat between them.

A telltale wetness gathered at the corner of her eyes, and

the overwhelming rush of feelings—joy, disbelief—pressed against her throat.

Slowly, she nodded, her voice quivering. "Yes," she whispered, then louder, with more certainty, "A thousand times, yes."

His arms encircled her as though he were incapable of enduring another minute of their separation. His lips grazed her temple, then her forehead, before finding her mouth in a kiss that expressed every unsaid word, every unspoken fear.

When they pulled apart, breathless, Emma let out a shaky laugh. "You really want this? To be here with me?" Her eyes searched his face for any trace of doubt.

His fingertips found the curve of her jaw, a whisper of contact that spoke volumes. "Watching you these past weeks … seeing your strength, your heart—made me realize that nothing else will ever come close to what I feel here, with you." His voice quieted, reverence lacing each word. "You are my dream, Emma."

Any last thoughts or reservations retreated, leaving only the sound of her quickened breathing.

"I can't imagine Sweetwater Springs—or my life—without you," she said. Her hands framed his well-defined features as if anchoring him to this moment.

She glanced outside. Tendrils of fog embraced the buildings; the streets hugged in a magical stillness.

As their lips met once more, the life she'd assumed she'd lost was right here, in his arms, unfolding in wonderful ways she'd never dared to imagine.

Another mystery of Sweetwater Springs was solved, its secrets uncovered, but for Emma and Victor, their story—their greatest adventure—was only beginning.

EPILOGUE - ONE YEAR LATER

The Sweetwater Springs Inn stood elegantly against the slate gray January sky, its weathered clapboard etched against the backdrop of towering firs and cedars.

Raindrops pattered against the frosted windowpanes, creating a quiet percussion. The lush, sonorous tones of a string quartet filtered through the inn's walls, their rendition of *Winter* from Vivaldi's Four Seasons was a nod to the season.

Inside the great room, flickering flames from the massive river rock fireplace cast dancing shadows across the rough-hewn beams overhead. The scent of cedar and mulled cider created a comforting balm against the Pacific Northwest chill.

Garlands of fragrant pine and fir cascaded along the banisters, accented by clusters of hellebores and delicate snowdrops—nature's bold rebellion against winter's grip.

At the far end of the room, an arch of twisted branches stood decked with sprays of witch hazel and early blooming camellias, their pale petals a whisper of the spring to come.

Wedding guests huddled in small groups, their conversations an array of murmurs and laughter. Crystal glasses clinked, and the rustle of finery added texture to the auditory landscape. The polished hardwood floors creaked occasionally underfoot, each sound a reminder of the inn's history as a gathering place for the community.

As twilight deepened, the glow of vintage Edison bulbs strung overhead intensified, bathing the room in a rich, amber light. The atmosphere crackled with an almost tangible energy—a collective holding of breath before the evening's main event.

Beneath a second arch twined with grape leaves and fairy lights, Emma stood beside Victor, her hand clasped in his. Pastor David, his Bible open before him, presided over the ceremony with a gentle gravitas that hushed the very air around them. Every moment seemed suspended in time; their whispered vows resonated with a depth that only the two of them fully understood.

Emma's white satin gown hugged her curves before flowing into a modest train. The treasured silver bracelet featuring a charm etched with the image of a lighthouse that Victor had gifted her for Christmas, encircled her wrist. Her bouquet, a cascade of snow-white anemones and sprigs of purple-flowered rosemary, symbolized remembrance and untold possibilities.

Victor cut a dashing figure in a charcoal gray suit, tailored to accentuate his broad shoulders. A sprig of wild huckleberry tucked into his lapel complemented the deep purple accents in Emma's bouquet, an understated tribute to the Pacific Northwest forests where they'd often hiked this past year. The berry's leaves, tinged with a winter burgundy, conveyed resilience and the promise of sweeter days ahead.

Pastor David's resonant voice spoke of covenant, of two becoming one in the eyes of God. His words, steeped in Scripture yet personalized for the couple before him, wove together themes of forgiveness, perseverance, and divine love.

As Emma and Victor's lips met, sealing a bond that had endured storms and uncertainty, the room erupted in applause. Delilah's sequined bodice and iridescent silk skirt created a mesmerizing display with each movement. Daintily, she dabbed at the corner of her eyes with a monogrammed handkerchief. Beside her, Gus pulled her close, a proud smile lighting his face.

The reception unfolded in the inn's banquet hall. Long tables of reclaimed wood, polished to a lustrous sheen, hosted mismatched vintage china and mason jars filled with fragrant sprigs of greenery.

Emma's pastries commanded attention from a central table, a tiered display of rustic elegance. Golden-crusted pies nestled next to sweet and chewy macaroons in hues of pink, blue, and purple. A tower of cinnamon-dusted churros stood beside crystallized flower-topped cupcakes, in lieu of a wedding cake.

Guests mingled, their laughter harmonizing with the strains of the quartet tucked into a comfortable alcove. The aroma of freshly brewed coffee wafted from a corner where Lillian Weatherly, her silver hair coiled in an elegant updo, presided over a gleaming copper urn with Theodore by her side.

James McAllister oversaw a board game area with newfound confidence, his eyes alight with enthusiasm as he explained rules and offered strategy tips. The rustle of cards brought bursts of laughter from guests gathered around tables laden with a selection of classic chess sets and modern party games.

Nearby, Mr. McAllister, his hair neatly combed and a smile crinkling the corners of his eyes, patiently taught a group of children the finer points of Monopoly. His solid hands helped little fingers count colorful bills, his encouraging voice carrying stories of activities from his own childhood.

Mrs. McAllister, resplendent in a vibrant red dress, flitted between tables with the grace of a hostess born. She offered words of encouragement to struggling players, topped up glasses of sparkling cider, and occasionally cast proud glances at James, her eyes misty with joy at seeing her son in his element.

Emma and Victor stepped to the center of the room for their first dance, *My Heart Will Go On*, by James Horner, and she glanced around. Sheriff Randall looked unusually at ease, sharing a quiet joke with Olivia and Daniel Whitfield. In a secluded corner, Elliot Fitzwater sat beside his wife, Nora, their quiet smiles a testament to their love. Emma overheard the couple discussing maple groves and refining the recipe for their trademark maple syrup.

Victor's voice brushed against her ear, soft and full of promise. "Are you happy, Raindrop?"

Emma turned to him, her chest swelling with emotion as she nestled her head against his shoulder. "More than I ever imagined."

When the music ended, Delilah's laughter rang out, her glass raised high. "Who's ready for my new song?" she asked.

Emma and Victor, as well as all the guests, clapped and chuckled, though no one seemed eager enough to volunteer for the first listen.

"Did you bring your ukelele?" Victor teased.

"Not tonight."

"Let's wait, then, Aunt Delilah," Elliot called out to her. "You can serenade me …. tomorrow."

Laughter rippled through the room, and Elliot leaned back in his chair with a smirk. Victor shot Emma a playful glance, both grateful they'd sidestepped Delilah's impromptu show—at least for the moment.

When the reception reached its peak, Emma and Victor excused themselves to change out of their wedding attire. Emma emerged from the bridal suite in a blue sweater dress, layered over warm leggings. She'd swapped her heels for sturdy, stylish ankle boots. A cashmere wrap, in a soft blush tone, draped around her shoulders, while a tailored navy-blue long coat added an elegant touch. A delicate gold leaf barrette, a gift from Delilah, replaced her intricate updo.

Victor traded his formal suit for dark jeans and a cable-knit pullover. He donned a canvas jacket, its collar turned up against the awaiting chill.

Hand-in-hand, they bid farewell to their guests, accepting final hugs and well-wishes. The newlyweds slipped out the side door of the inn, the sounds of celebration diminishing behind them as they stepped onto Main Street.

Emma's boots clicked on the sidewalk, while Victor's footsteps kept a steady rhythm beside her. Their breaths blended in the chilly air, a soft veil between them, much like the future they were weaving together.

"Can you believe how much has changed in only a year?" she mused.

He chuckled. "Tell me about it. From you battling your hoarding tendencies to completely renovating the bakery. How does it feel to have a clutter-free kitchen and apartment?"

"Liberating. Terrifying. But mostly amazing. Remember when you helped me sort through those boxes of old receipts?"

"How could I forget? That's when my accounting skills truly came in handy. Speaking of which, this year has been quite the ride for me, too."

Emma nodded. "From dreaming of the FBI to where you are now. How's the cybersecurity work going?"

"Challenging in the best way. My knack for numbers has translated well into tracking digital footprints. Sheriff Randall and his entire police department have been calling me their secret weapon in fighting online fraud."

"My heroic number-cruncher," Emma laughed, bumping his shoulder. "To think, it all started with you helping Elliot solve the embezzlement mystery."

"Life has a funny way of opening doors, doesn't it?" Victor said. "One minute I'm searching for a lighthouse that has been gone for decades, the next I'm advising on cyberse-curity for half the businesses in this and surrounding towns."

She grinned. "We've both come so far. Me, facing my fears and letting go of the past. And you are protecting people without having to leave Sweetwater Springs."

"So, Mrs. Steele, what's next?"

"I want to check on *Blissful Bites*—Alice Lancaster baked an extra batch of snickerdoodles for tomorrow."

"Are you expecting a large crowd of customers?"

"Hopefully. Certainly, James McAllister and Dr. George Carter will stop in. Both have shown a keen interest in her. She's in her thirties and really pretty—wavy chestnut hair and those amazing hazel eyes that light up when she smiles."

He laughed, shaking his head. "Today is our wedding day, Emma. Certainly, the bakery, and any budding romances, can wait."

"She's my new hire, and snickerdoodles are my trademark cookie recipe. She brings a spark to the shop with her creativity and enthusiasm. I want to see if she added anything different to the cookies."

"I'm sure they're delicious."

Emma grinned up at him. "I'll only pop in for a few minutes, I promise."

He checked his watch. "That'll give me time to get something."

"Get what?"

He grinned. "You'll see."

True to her word, Emma locked the bakery fifteen minutes later. Alice had baked and then stored the cookies in airtight containers, and she hadn't changed a thing.

Emma stepped away, and a gust of wind cut through her coat, replacing the brown butter and cinnamon scents of the snickerdoodles with January's sharp bite.

By the curb, Victor leaned against his parked car, hands tucked into his pockets. He rocked slightly on his heels, his gaze darting between Emma and a paper bag on the car's hood. When she drew near, he cleared his throat, failing to suppress a chuckle as he grasped for the bag with exaggerated casualness.

"That's what you had to get? Your car?" she asked. "What are you up to?"

He shrugged and handed her the bag, nearly dropping its contents in his eagerness. "Open it," he urged, his voice pitched slightly higher than usual.

She reached inside, withdrawing a glossy travel book. She flipped through it, revealing crisp pages filled with Italian phrases.

"You want me to learn Italian?"

"Why not?" He grinned and opened the car door. "Get in. We're going for a drive."

"Where?" She hesitated, smiling despite herself. "Everything is perfect, Victor. What could make this night any better?"

He kissed her, his breath warm against her neck. "Almost perfect. There's something else."

"Victor, as you just reminded me, this is our wedding day."

"The airport is only an hour away." A grin spread across his face. Before she could respond, he produced two slips of paper from his jacket pocket. In the streetlamp's glow, plane tickets with the words "Seattle to Venice" were clearly visible.

The travel book slipped from her fingers, landing on the floor of the car.

Emma gasped. "Venice? But ... how? When?"

"Now. Our flight leaves in three hours."

"Now?" Emma's voice rose an octave. "We haven't packed, my bakery—"

"All taken care of," Victor assured. "Alice is handling the bakery, and there's two suitcases for each of us in the trunk. I may have had some help from Delilah."

"May have? You planned all this? A surprise honeymoon, leaving tonight?"

He nodded. "I always talked about wanting you to see Italy. I figured, why wait?"

Emma threw her arms around his neck. "You're incredible, you know that?"

"Only because I have you," he replied, holding her close. "Shall we head to the airport? Venice awaits, Mrs. Steele."

Emma laughed, a sound of pure joy. "Lead the way, Mr. Steele."

As they drove, the recognizable silhouettes of Sweetwater Springs receded in the rearview mirror. A fine mist clung to the windshield, the wipers keeping a steady rhythm against the drizzle. Droplets raced down Emma's window, their paths illuminated by passing headlights.

"I always thought the magic of Sweetwater Springs was in the town itself," she murmured. "Now I see it differently."

He glanced at her. "How so?"

"It's not the place. It's the connections, the people. In moments like this one."

He reached over, his hand finding hers. "We're taking a bit of that magic with us to Venice."

She nodded, her heart full. As they drove on toward their next adventure, she knew that no matter where life took them, they'd always carry a piece of Sweetwater Springs in their hearts.

Two days later, the gentle sway of water lapping against the stone walls of Venice pulled Emma from her dreams. Sunlight filtered through the gauzy curtains, creating shifting hues on the ornate frescoes overhead. Victor slept beside her, his face peaceful.

Smiling, she slipped out of bed and padded to the balcony. The Grand Canal stretched before her, a ribbon of deep blues and greens, dotted with gondolas gliding past weathered palazzos. The magic of Venice was palpable in every quiet breath she took.

"Buongiorno, bella," Victor's husky voice came from behind her as he wrapped his arms around her waist.

She leaned into him, her heart expanding. "This city seems like a dream."

The day unfurled in a way only Venice could provide— getting lost in the streets that wove together in a delightful maze, discovering hidden corners filled with centuries-old charm. They shared cicchetti in a tiny bacaro, the taste of prosciutto and melon a perfect contrast to the crisp Prosecco.

They crossed the Rialto Bridge, and Emma couldn't deny the thrill that bubbled inside her. Venice was a city steeped in history, its tales encircling every shadowed alley and ancient facade.

Later, as their gondola glided through a quiet canal at sunset, Victor lifted his antique camera, framing the breath-taking view of the sun dipping below the horizon. The golden light danced across the water, and he smiled as he captured the moment.

"This is perfect," he murmured, lowering the camera and turning to her. "I have something for you."

She looked up. "What is it?"

He reached into his bag, retrieving an elegantly wrapped box tied with a silver ribbon. "Open it," he urged, a smile spreading across his face.

She unwrapped the box, revealing a collection of photographs. Each image was carefully mounted, and she gasped as she recognized the familiar shapes of cherished items—her mother's rolling pins, an ornate teapot, and the delicate porcelain figurines from her childhood.

"Victor, how did you …?" she trailed off, overwhelmed.

"I took the liberty of photographing the things you planned to donate," he explained. "I wanted you to have a piece of your past, something to hold onto as you let go of the physical items."

"This is incredible. I can't believe you did this for me. Thank you. They're beautiful." Tears welled as she kissed him, his devotion surrounding her like a loving embrace.

"Every picture tells a story," he said. "While it's important to move forward, it's equally important to remember where you came from." He wrapped an arm around her, holding her close. She nestled into his side, lost in thought, her heart full but her mind swirling with the memories the photographs evoked.

After a moment of comfortable silence, he tilted his head to look at her, concern softening his gaze. "What's going on in that lovely mind of yours, Raindrop?"

She gazed out at the gleaming lights reflecting on the canal. "I was thinking about Sweetwater Springs, and how it's more than a place. It's … a feeling. And that feeling extends beyond a spot on a map."

He kissed her forehead. "True. And now Venice awaits us."

As they drifted off later that night, contentment settled over Emma, as comforting as it was exhilarating. The essence of Sweetwater Springs wasn't confined to its quaint streets or snow-capped mountains. It lived in the quiet moments, in the shared laughter, in the way Victor's hand found hers in the dark.

She turned to gaze at her husband, his features softened by the moonlight streaming through the window. Threads of home and adventure, of the familiar and the unknown, wove love together.

Sleep beckoned, and her last thoughts were of the journey ahead. With Victor by her side, every cobblestone street and hidden canal held the promise of discovery. The true magic of life lay not in grand gestures but in the everyday miracles of love freely given and joyfully received.

The whisper of Sweetwater Springs' charm hadn't faded with distance—it pulsed between heartbeats, in the quiet understanding that passed between her and Victor without words.

Between wakefulness and dreams, Emma began to truly understand that the true marvel of life transcended geography. Life and love lived in stolen glances, shared laughter, and infinite possibilities.

As dawn broke, Emma nudged Victor from his slumber.

"What if we bring a piece of Venice back to Sweetwater Springs?" she whispered excitedly.

Victor blinked sleepily. "What do you mean?"

"A Venetian carnival! We could host it at the bakery with masks, Italian pastries, maybe even gondola rides on the lake."

He grinned, fully alert now. "*Blissful Bites* goes international. I like it."

Her mind swirled with possibilities. "We'll get everyone involved. Olivia can create an Italian literature display, Delilah can serenade us with Italian love songs …"

He chuckled. "I can already hear Delilah warming up her vocal cords."

A quiet, powerful joy took hold of her heart, picturing their town embracing a slice of Venetian charm.

Sweetwater Springs had always been home, but now it was more than that—a place where dreams took flight and whispers of holiday magic filled the air. It was brimming with possibilities, where love and the enchantment of any season would always find a way to endure.

THE END

RECIPE FOR SNICKERDOODLE COOKIES

Ingredients:

For the Cookies:

- 1 cup (2 sticks) unsalted butter
- 1 ½ cups granulated sugar
- 2 large eggs
- 1 tsp vanilla extract
- 2 ¾ cups all-purpose flour
- 1 ½ tsp cream of tartar
- 1 tsp baking soda
- ½ tsp ground cinnamon

- ¼ tsp salt

For the Cinnamon-Sugar Coating:

- ¼ cup granulated sugar
- 1 ½ tsp ground cinnamon

Instructions:

1. **Brown the Butter:**
   - In a medium saucepan, melt the butter over medium heat, stirring occasionally. Continue cooking until the butter turns golden brown and starts to release a nutty aroma (about 5-7 minutes). Watch closely to avoid burning.
   - Once browned, pour the butter into a heatproof bowl and let it cool to room temperature.
2. **Make the Dough:**
   - In a large mixing bowl, combine the cooled browned butter and granulated sugar. Beat together until well combined.
   - Add the eggs one at a time, followed by the vanilla extract, and mix until smooth and creamy.
   - In a separate bowl, whisk together the flour, cream of tartar, baking soda, cinnamon, and salt.
   - Gradually add the dry ingredients to the wet mixture, stirring until the dough comes together. It will be slightly thick and sticky.
3. **Chill the Dough:**
   - Cover the dough and refrigerate for at least 30 minutes (or up to 2 hours) to allow the flavors

to meld and to firm up the dough for easy rolling.

4. **Preheat the Oven:**
   - While the dough chills, preheat your oven to 350°F (175°C). Line baking sheets with parchment paper or silicone baking mats.

5. **Prepare the Cinnamon-Sugar Coating:**
   - In a small bowl, mix the granulated sugar and cinnamon for the coating.

6. **Shape the Cookies:**
   - Roll the chilled dough into 1.5-inch balls (about 1 tablespoon of dough per ball). Roll each ball in the cinnamon-sugar mixture, ensuring an even coating.

7. **Bake the Cookies:**
   - Place the dough balls onto the prepared baking sheets, spacing them about 2 inches apart.
   - Bake for 9-11 minutes, or until the edges are set and the tops are slightly crackled. The centers may look a little soft but will firm up as they cool.

8. **Cool and Serve:**
   - Let the cookies cool on the baking sheet for 5 minutes, then transfer to a wire rack to cool completely.

Enjoy your **Snickerdoodle Cookies with Browned Butter and Cinnamon**! These cookies are soft, chewy, and full of warm cinnamon spice with a hint of nutty richness from the browned butter. Perfect for any occasion!

A NOTE FROM JOSIE

Dear Reader,

Thank you for reading *Whispers of Holiday Magic in Sweetwater Springs*, the third book in the beloved Sweetwater Springs series. This cozy mystery romance takes you deeper into the heart of our charming Pacific Northwest town, where secrets simmer beneath the surface and holiday magic works in mysterious ways.

In this story, we explore the power of facing our fears and embracing change. Emma's journey from a woman trapped by her past to one ready to seize her future mirrors the town's own evolution. Victor's quest to solve a financial mystery becomes a catalyst for personal growth and unexpected love.

The theme of community shines brightly in this novel. As Emma and Victor work to uncover long-buried truths, they discover the strength that comes from standing together. The colorful cast of Sweetwater Springs residents - from the mischievous Delilah to the steadfast Sheriff Randall - reminds us that family isn't always bound by blood, but by the connections we forge.

Baking plays a central role in this story, serving as both Emma's passion and a metaphor for life. Just as a perfect recipe requires balance and patience, so too does love and personal growth. Emma's delicious creations will inspire you to find joy in the simple pleasures of home and hearth.

As you turn the final page, I hope you'll feel the warmth of new beginnings, the excitement of solving a good mystery, and the comfort of finding where you truly belong.

May Emma and Victor's story remind you that sometimes the most precious gifts come in unexpected packages, wrapped in whispers of holiday magic.

Thank you for continuing this journey with me through Sweetwater Springs.

Warmest wishes,
  Josie Riviera

P.S. I'd love to hear your thoughts! Please feel free to reach out to me on social media or via email to share your feedback, ask questions, or just say hello. Connecting with readers is one of the greatest joys of being an author, and I'm always thrilled to hear from you.

Whispers of Holiday Magic in Sweetwater Springs is available in ebook, paperback, Large Print paperback, audiobook, and Hardcover.

P.S.S. As I write my next sweet or inspirational romance, remember this: Have you ever tried something you were afraid to try because it mattered so much to you? I did, when I started writing. Take the chance, and just do something you love.

Love music?

My Spotify list for Whispers of Holiday Magic in Sweetwater Springs is here.

CHAPTER ONE

"You've got to be kidding me! Only two boxes of books when I ordered three?" Olivia Harper's exasperated voice echoed through the cozy confines of *Harper's Haven*, the bookshop she'd inherited from her grandfather Elijah.

She hoisted the books inside and shook her head. "I guess I'll have to charm my customers with my dazzling personality instead of relying on the books."

With a grin and a sigh, she reached for her cell phone to rectify the mistake. Sunlight filtered through the lace curtains, casting a glow over the antique furniture and overstuffed chairs. The scent of aged paper and rich mahogany embraced her like an old friend.

Blooming cherry blossom trees, with slender upright branches and rounded canopies, lined the street. When she finished her phone call, she opened the window to let in the floral-scented air.

As she gazed around her shop, a flicker of uncertainty passed through her.

Harper's Haven wasn't just a bookstore—it was her dream, her legacy. She had poured her heart and soul into every detail, determined to carry on her grandfather's proud tradition. But lately, the weight of responsibility seemed more burdensome than ever.

With each passing year, the pressures of running the business grew more daunting.

She shrugged off her khaki-colored windbreaker, hung it on a hook by the door, and secured an apron over her clothes. Then she kneeled beside the book shipments and sliced through the packing tape.

She lifted out two hardbound editions of *Wuthering Heights*, their gold-leaf lettering glinting in the gauzy morning light.

The distinct tinkle of the shop bell was unmistakable, and she greeted the first customer of the day.

But no one responded.

"Hello?" she called out again. "Can I help you find anything?"

Only silence. Every aisle lay empty and still.

Okay, this was strange. She was certain she had heard the bell.

"Anyone here?" She repeated.

Nope. No reply. She must've been mistaken. She was obviously alone.

Corralling her unease into something more productive, she redirected her attention to her task. As she sliced through the packing tape on the next box, a flash of creamy parchment grabbed her attention. She crouched for a better look, clearing dust bunnies from the wooden floorboards. An envelope lay slightly hidden underneath the front door.

She yanked the envelope free. The texture was luxuriously thick, and clearly expensive stationery. No postage, no address … only a wax seal, keeping its contents mysteriously confined. The wax itself was an unusual shade of yellow, its sheen catching the morning light streaming through the windows.

There were no clues as to the sender, an intriguing omission.

Her fingertip dipped over fancy lettering.

The initials L.B.

Where had she seen that unique script before, with its elongated curves and artistic loops? It tugged at her memory but hovered slightly out of reach.

The letter was addressed to:

Ms. Lillian Beaumont

Sweetwater Springs

Whispers of Love

"Whispers of love?" she asked aloud. "What does it mean?"

The handwritten style was antiquated but graceful, with

long, sweeping strokes. All perfectly precise except for the initial L, elongated by a slight wavering in an otherwise steady hand.

As Olivia flipped the envelope, a tiny drawing made her breath still. A single heart flanked Lillian's name, colored a vivid red.

Lillian Beaumont was a woman in her 70s. She had recently moved back to Sweetwater Springs, having been gone for decades. Elegant and from an esteemed family, she lived on her inherited estate at the edge of town.

Her silver hair was always perfectly styled. She favored classic pieces in luxurious fabrics—cashmere sweaters in soft pastels, pencil skirts, and her signature red lipstick. On occasion, she perused Olivia's bookshop and purchased armfuls of classic books.

Although, come to think of it, Olivia hadn't seen Lillian in several weeks.

She straightened.

In her peripheral vision, she caught a flicker of motion behind her—the swish of a coat, an odd shuffle of footsteps quickly fading.

Envelope still in hand, she wandered down the aisle.

"Hello? May I help you find anything?"

Again, nothing. The silence seemed to press in on her, heavy and unsettling.

She retreated and ran her fingertip over the wax seal, specks of it breaking off, then placed the envelope on the counter.

As she unloaded the remaining shipments, her thoughts drifted to the unexplained letter. Who was it from, and why deliver it in such a cryptic way? The hand-drawn heart suggested Lillian had a secret admirer.

The morning passed quickly with a steady stream of

customers, while Olivia dusted off shelves, lit several scented candles, and cashed out book sales.

The sunny spring weather had apparently put everyone in high spirits and in a buying mood. She helped Mrs. Dalton select a few gardening books to start planning her summer vegetable garden. She also set aside a couple of new young adult fantasy novels for two teenage girls to pick up.

At noon, Emma Jacobsen, who owned *Blissful Bites*, the bakery next door, stopped by. As usual, she was dressed to the nines despite her flour-dusted apron. Emma often came to chat when business was slow. She was in her late twenties, with fair skin and glowing, rosy cheeks.

"I'm done for the day and headed home," Emma announced. Her blond hair fell to her shoulders in loose waves, impervious to frizz or the hairnet she often wore.

"You sold all of your baked goods already?" Olivia asked.

"Every single one, but I saved a chocolate donut for you." Emma handed Olivia a donut wrapped in wax paper.

"Thank you and enjoy the rest of your afternoon," Olivia smiled. "I don't close until six o'clock."

"But I start preparing fresh dough and baking before sunrise, so I work more hours than you."

"I don't know about that." Olivia gave Emma a mischievous jab and took a bite of her donut, thinking about the extra hours she spent on inventory management and curating book selections.

In her typical brazen fashion, Emma's gaze flew to the envelope on the counter. "What ... do we have here?" Her tone shifted to a higher pitch.

While Olivia recounted the story, an almost imperceptible shift appeared in her friend's appearance.

Emma grimaced and touched her neck. "Possibly it's one of Lillian's secret fans." She shifted from one foot to the other. "You always had a knack for solving puzzles when we were young. I'm sure you'll be able to figure it out."

"Lillian Beaumont hasn't dated in ages. Word is, she never married."

"It's never too late for love." Emma's shoulders hunched. "At least for you. Not for me."

"Don't say that."

"I'm still struggling to run the bakery after my mother's passing. That's enough excitement for me."

"You have the option to hire help to reduce your workload," Olivia replied.

"Like you? You've never done anything of the sort."

Olivia shrugged. "I'm fine."

"So am I, and I'll run the bakery alone. My mother and grandmother did, and I'm carrying on their legacy."

A legacy of overwork, Olivia thought, though she kept silent. Emma wouldn't trust her bakery to anyone else. Her grief over her mother's unexpected death had stopped her from moving forward with her life.

Olivia grabbed a bottle of water from behind the counter and drank several sips. "So, you and I are currently dateless."

"Seems that way."

In truth, Olivia longed for a partner, a man to share her passions and support her dreams. She yearned for the warmth of love and the comfort of a family. However, exactly like Emma, fear held her back. Fear of change, fear of letting someone in, fear of losing the one constant in her life —her cherished bookshop.

"Maybe a handsome, heroic guy will move into town for you," Emma said.

"He better move in soon." Olivia smiled. "Or at least before I hit the age of thirty."

"Hey, if it's not too late for Lillian, then it's definitely not too late for you." Emma tapped her fingers on the counter. Nevertheless, there was more to her words—something lurking just below the surface. "The letter writer might be someone closer than you think."

As they swapped speculations, Emma's attentiveness carried a deliberate edge as she adjusted her denim skirt and fidgeted with her hair.

Did she know something? Or was she merely playing along with the intrigue?

Though they contrasted in looks, with Emma's petite frame and blond locks differing from Olivia's willowy height and chestnut curls, their friendship had always worked. As different as sunrise and sunset, each woman admired talents in the other she herself did not possess, and, despite her odd behavior, Emma was a true and reliable friend.

With a quick goodbye, Emma headed back to her bakery to close for the day, with promises to sleuth out ideas about the letter writer.

Although the bookshop kept Olivia busy for the next hour, her thoughts took a detour. Underneath her cheerful demeanor, a deep longing for companionship and love had taken root. She wanted someone to share her experiences, her interests, and the quiet moments that made life worth living.

Work had become her sanctuary, a refuge where she had the opportunity to lose herself in stories, and vicariously experience the affection she craved. Yet, as fulfilling as her work was, it was unable to fill the void in her heart.

Love would require a leap of faith, a willingness to risk her carefully cultivated independence, and take a chance. The alternative—a life spent alone witnessing others discover their happily-ever-afters—seemed increasingly hollow.

Shaking off her melancholy thoughts, she resumed the task at hand. She couldn't help but wonder if the mysterious letter held a clue to Lillian's own journey with love. Perhaps, in unraveling the secrets of the past, Olivia might stumble upon the courage to open her heart to the possibilities of the future.

She looked forward to catching up with Lillian. The woman's wit and sophistication always brightened Olivia's day.

Should she notify her about the strange delivery?

Yes, of course. The letter was addressed to her, and the contents were none of Olivia's business. She should personally deliver the letter to Lillian.

Then again, maybe not. Olivia sought to respect the privacy of the letter's sender as well as that of the recipient. More importantly, directly approaching Lillian without understanding the context or the sender's intentions could be intrusive.

Olivia ran her fingers across the weighty parchment. The meticulously drawn heart suggested strong emotions.

When the time was right, she'd approach Lillian in a thoughtful and considerate manner, planning the conversation to ensure a positive and supportive interaction.

She tucked the letter in her apron pocket for safekeeping and decided to observe Lillian closely at their next meeting before springing the letter on her. Perhaps there would be unspoken clues—a blush, a tearful glimmer in her eye—to expose whether joyous news or old heartaches might wait within the envelope. For now, the contents remained unknown.

The shop bell jangled, and the front door swung open.

Olivia looked up, a greeting frozen on her lips.

Her childhood friend stood in the doorway, his hazel eyes glinting beneath his artfully tousled dark hair.

She grabbed the counter to steady herself, hoping her knees wouldn't give out.

"Daniel Whitfield. Is it really you?" The question ran from her lips. Her pulse thumped in her ears, resembling an erratic drumbeat. She studied his handsome face, searching for traces of the boy she had once known.

Their gazes locked, and the seconds hung suspended. His athletic build and broad shoulders filled out a well-fitted leather jacket. His wavy hair framed a face that had grown more chiseled and defined since their teenage years.

He summoned images of long ago afternoons spent sharing books, floating into imaginary worlds, and eating chocolate-chip cookies. Her favorite, she'd declared. Especially if they had lots of chocolate chips.

"Loads," he always assured her when he handed her a store-bought cookie. His grin suggested that he might've sneaked in a few extra chips when she wasn't looking.

Daniel had been her best friend and appreciated her shy introspection.

He got her. He understood her.

They passed countless summer evenings chasing fireflies and stargazing, dreaming about the lives they would someday lead.

When they grew into their teens, she developed an insatiable crush on him. She thought of him always and everywhere, even when they weren't together. She assumed he felt the same when they shared their first kiss.

But then he was gone, awarded a scholarship to a prestigious college in another state, aspiring to become a historian and preservationist specializing in museum studies.

"I'm planning to travel the world, Ollie," he told her. "But someday I'll be back."

And she was left in Sweetwater Springs. Alone. And he hadn't come back.

He promised to stay in touch, though he never had, save for a few postcards and hasty letters.

Seeing him in person after all these years, his unexpected appearance only amplified the warring emotions inside her.

His achievements in international projects that integrated history and preservation techniques had led to frequent media appearances. She'd seen his interviews on television and online.

"Hi," he said quietly. He stepped further into the shop, and anticipation fluttered in her chest. His presence filled the room, commanding, yet reassuring, like a warm cuddle on a chilly day. He came closer, his gaze never leaving hers. "You look great."

She fine-tuned the buttons on her cream blouse. She had paired the blouse with a floral skirt, accessorized by Grandma Rachel's pearl necklace. Classic clothing in the old Hollywood style suited her better than mass produced modern fashion. The styles had histories. Similar to her books.

Though today she didn't feel stylish. Today, she felt self-conscious.

Perhaps, if she was well-traveled.

But she wasn't, and he was.

"Thanks. You're not so bad yourself." She felt a blushing warmth travel up her cheeks, and she silently hoped that the sunlight through the window wouldn't betray her reaction to his closeness.

Sporting his signature crooked smile, he embraced her in a long, tender hug. His masculine scent mixed with leather and an intoxicating foreign spice—something new and spicy —and more evidence of the success she'd admired from afar.

She inhaled traces of the familiar, clean, and fresh, uniquely him. It brought back a flood of memories, of stolen kisses and whispered promises of a love that had never faded.

The strength of his arms offered security, a quiet acknowledgement of the years they'd spent apart. She pressed her face into his chest, unable to resist, and noticed his heart quickening ever so slightly.

"It's so good to see you, Ollie," he murmured in her ear, sending a tingle down her spine. "Real, real good." His hands rested on her shoulders, igniting memories of their long-held connection.

Ollie. The nickname was a nod to their shared history, an affectionate shorthand, like slipping into a well-worn pair of shoes. He hadn't forgotten.

She met his hazel eyes, reflecting intelligence, kindness, and longing. Tiny flecks of gold danced in their depths. And something more—a hidden gravity she couldn't fully decipher.

"You haven't called me Ollie since we were kids." She swept back a chestnut curl escaping from her updo, silently cursing her unruly hair for choosing this moment to stage a rebellion.

"Concrete proof it's been far too long." His eyes twinkled with mirth, though his voice was low and smooth. "I hope you haven't outgrown your affection for socks that don't match."

"Never," she replied.

Once upon a time, they confessed things to each other. He once had a dream of being able to fly, so real that he'd been disappointed when he woke up and realized it wasn't true. She always wore mismatched socks for good luck, and it had become a personal superstition.

Today she wore one red and one blue sock. Some superstitions died hard.

Affection enveloped her from head to toe as she soaked in his good-looking features. His face carried a touch of rugged individuality, and his jawline was peppered with a dark stubble that lent him an air of casual sophistication. The radiance of his smile had the power to brighten even the darkest corners of her heart.

Time had certainly changed everything. In the past, he was her confidante.

But now. Now things were different—even more intimate.

"I've returned to settle down in this town permanently." He lifted her chin. "Are you pleased?"

She studied his face, searching for the boy she had once known. She took in the man he had become, a heady mix of awareness and novelty that left her both exhilarated and unbalanced. "If your words hold true, then undoubtedly."

"They are true." The curve of his lips radiated genuine understanding. "Think you can catch me up on things around Sweetwater Springs?" He gestured toward the door. "Possibly over lunch?"

"I already ate a chocolate donut."

"A donut isn't lunch."

"For me, it is, though I might be able to clear my schedule for an old friend on a different day."

"I plan to be more than an old friend." As he scanned a shelf of historical fiction, his hand covered hers, where it rested on the polished oak surface of the counter. "Remember when we said we'd marry each other if we weren't able to find anyone better?"

"We used to joke about it. So, you didn't hit the jackpot?"

"Nope. You?"

"Nope." Her stomach fluttered, and she quickly changed the subject as she gazed across her shop—anywhere but at him. Every corner held a piece of her heart, from the eclectic array of books to the elegant retro seating.

"What brings you here today?" she asked.

"You."

"Me? I'm hardly a jackpot." She laughed, a bit too loudly. "You moved back to Sweetwater Springs several weeks ago."

"Ah, you've been checking up on me?"

"No."

Well, yes. In this modest town of ten thousand, news waltzed faster than the eye could blink.

"I was busy buying a house on Windsor Boulevard," he said. "An old Victorian."

"Ooh. Quite a posh street." Her comment carried a hint of good-humored recognition, a nod to the world they had once dreamed about.

Daniel chuckled. "Windsor Boulevard seemed fitting. A bit different from the old neighborhood."

Olivia detected a blend of ambition and desire in his words.

"You did it," she said. Despite his humble upbringing, he'd continually expressed a wish to reside on a more affluent street.

"Right." He shifted. "Like I mentioned, I came here to see you. Plus, I met with the historical society about an upcoming exhibition, and it's only a half block away."

"Don't put yourself out."

He grinned. His hand still covered hers. His other hand reached for a leather-bound book on a shelf near the counter. "Hey, your shop is incredible—a reading corner and a brass chandelier. You've upgraded since your grandfather owned it."

Her shop wasn't solely a bookstore; it was a charming haven, nestled in the heart of Sweetwater Springs. Whenever she stepped inside, she marveled at how it always felt like coming home.

Visions of couples browsing the shelves for romantic reads, snuggled in the leather armchairs by the fireplace, brought a smile to her face. The antique volumes, with their tales of adventure, mystery, and timeless love, never failed to cast their spell over everyone who loved to read.

"Thanks. A lot can happen in ten years." Olivia drew back her hand. "You're welcome to look around. I have a fiction section and a shelf full of thriller novels."

She gestured to a reading nook nestled between two towering bookcases and studied his profile when he turned. Sunlight from the front window glinted off his dark, tousled hair, the color of espresso. His eyes glittered with an inquisitive spark, which she recalled from their childhood adventures scouring the countryside for magical creatures drawn from fairy tales. Whether in Sweetwater Springs or abroad, his lively imagination had led him to pursue a career safeguarding the rich history and architecture of the past.

After he slid a worn Agatha Christie book onto a shelf, he turned fully toward her, his desire softening his gaze.

Her breath snagged as his fingers swept away a stray wisp of hair that had fallen across her cheek. That rebellious hair again.

His fleeting touch had sparks leaping over her skin. She looked down, suddenly fascinated by the intricate pattern of the hardwood floor.

"I'm glad we finally have a chance to catch up, Ollie."

"Me, too." She missed him. His return was like a sucker punch to the gut, so unexpected yet so wonderful, and there was no hope for it.

"Do you remember the last time we saw each other?" he asked. "That summer evening by the lake, before I left for college?"

"How could I forget? We made a multitude of plans, dreamed endless dreams."

"I'm sorry it took me so long to return."

When she didn't respond, he stepped back and flipped through the pages of a well-known bestseller. "Remember when we used to go on treasure hunts?"

"Of course." She gave a slight dip of her head. "Or our hush-hush codes and messages?"

"Mirror writing. And our underground scripts and cipher pies."

"Definitely the best," she agreed.

"Are you keeping any secrets these days, Ollie?"

"Like what?"

"Any guy I should be aware of?" He pointedly stared at her left hand.

She was ringless.

"None. Though actually ..." Olivia debated whether to involve him in her discovery of the puzzling letter. His passion for discovering concealed artifacts might be beneficial.

She retrieved the envelope and recounted the peculiar delivery.

"Whispers of Love? It sounds like the title of a romantic poem. And the heart drawing. Perhaps the sender had a special connection to Lillian." Daniel examined the letter, noting the expensive stationery and calligraphy spelling of Lillian Beaumont's name. "I remember her well. She once caught us trying to sneak a peek at her famous rose garden. I worried that she'd never stop scolding us."

"We were quite the mischievous duo, weren't we? I'm surprised that she didn't ban us from her property forever."

"Have you spoken to her about the letter?"

"Not yet. I wanted to observe her first in case the contents were sensitive."

"I'd be happy to partner on your little investigation if you'll have me. For old time's sake?" His eyes held an adventurous sparkle that Olivia well remembered.

"I'd love that." She swallowed the lump in her throat for all the years that had gone by without him, then tucked the letter back in her apron pocket.

Some things never changed. Their enduring bond of friendship and comradery transcended time. They weren't only discussing solving a mystery, they were rediscovering their love of a shared undertaking.

As he turned to leave, promising to be in touch, the bell jingled, its ring unusually sharp and insistent.

They traded a startled look.

He yanked the door open, surveying the cobblestone sidewalk as Olivia joined him.

The town's postcard-perfect street stretched before them. Locally owned businesses were painted in earthy tones, complementing the natural beauty of the surroundings. Potted plants sat outside in vivid purple and pink colors, a stark contrast against the subdued architecture. Spring had arrived in the Pacific Northwest, awakening the scenic mountain community from its winter slumber.

This was her favorite season, when the promise of fresh beginnings wrapped her world in an optimistic glow.

A beam of sun struggled to pierce impenetrable clouds. Yet the street seemed frozen in a silent scene, as if the entire town had taken a collective pause. The only sounds were the occasional creak of a road sign or the hum of a far-off car engine.

Olivia twisted one of the pearls on her necklace, the smoothness comforting to the touch. "Where is everyone?" she whispered.

"At lunch?" Daniel half-joked, although his lips tightened. "Your shop bell rang, right?"

"I heard it as loudly as you did." Goosebumps prickled her skin despite the snug temperature of the bookshop. First the unexplained letter, now phantom bell ringers? This day was getting odder by the minute.

After his departure a few minutes later, Olivia busied herself tending to afternoon customers while mulling over potential clues. Every so often, her thoughts strayed to Daniel. His passion for discovering the buried stories of people, sometimes in precarious situations, mirrored her own love of books and mysteries.

She inhaled. The comforting mustiness of well-loved novels, the faint trace of vanilla-scented candles flickering on antique tables, added to the light floral fragrance of cherry blossoms drifting in through the open window. The scent always reminded her of almonds or marzipans.

Hours later, before she closed for the day, a final tinkling bell roused her as Mr. Theodore Weatherly ambled through the doorway. A distinguished face in Sweetwater Springs, Theodore had never married, vehemently asserting he preferred to live alone. He was a kindly retired poet, and well-known for his calm, observant nature, and talent for heartrending verses.

"Good evening, Olivia." Theodore's clear blue eyes creased behind his trademark round spectacles.

"I'm about ready to close," she reminded him, as she did every night around the same time.

"I know. I'm taking a stroll to catch the last rays and mingle with the night shadows. A little tango with the sunset and a potential chat with the neighborhood cats. Gotta keep these old bones in check." He chortled. "What are you up to?"

Olivia smiled at his characteristic whimsy; a fox-trot of words frequently accompanied his escapades.

With his shock of white hair, and an endless collection of colorful bow ties, he had a habit of strolling slowly while nodding approval of his surroundings, as if the town were his personal art gallery and he were the sole critic.

"Oh, I'm not up to much, Theodore." Olivia felt for Lillian's letter in her apron pocket. "Merely some intriguing mysteries to unfold."

Theodore swallowed hard, then waved a hand airily. "Ah yes, life does delight in its little enigmas." He trailed off, his eyes unfocusing as if lost in inflated memories.

"How well do know Lillian Beaumont?" she blurted.

"Ah … beautiful, delightful Lillian." A tender smile graced his lips. "I used to know her well before she moved away."

"She moved back."

"I heard." He nodded, and she detected a quiver in his voice.

She wondered, not for the first time, what forgotten stories from past decades revolved around his discerning mind. He didn't inquire about her intriguing mystery, and she didn't expand on it. Apparently, he wasn't interested.

After a short interval, his smile returned.

"Alright, good night." Theodore turned on his heel. "I'm gonna check on my daughter's bakery next door."

Although not his biological daughter, Emma had become Theodore's daughter in spirit, his only family over the years. On many occasions, they spent holidays together.

Olivia wished the scenario would eventually change for Emma, wished she would be able to heal from her mother's passing. It didn't mean Emma should exclude Theodore from her life. It simply meant that she needed a healthy relationship with a man she could love.

"Emma closed her bakery after lunch," Olivia replied.

"I'll catch her tomorrow, then." Theodore drifted out the door, humming a romantic melody.

I Love You More Today Than Yesterday.

Sonny & Cher? Spiral Staircase? Olivia recognized the song immediately.

Bemused, she watched him go.

Theodore couldn't have a connection to the letter, could he?

Dismissing the possibility, Olivia retrieved the envelope. She examined the handwriting once more, searching for any trace to jog her memory.

Nope. Not a thing.

For the next ten minutes, she shelved the last few books, reluctant for the inviting refuge of her bookstore to go dim and silent.

The shop bell rang again, louder than usual, a sudden disruption rippling through the bookshop.

"Hello?" She tried to listen for more. Sounds. Footsteps. Anything. "Theodore? Sorry, but remember, I'm about to close?"

No one stood in the doorway.

The fine hairs on her arms lifted, as if invaded by tiny pushpins. The tidy space looked undisturbed; the books were organized on their appropriate shelves. However, she couldn't escape the uncanny sensation of invisible eyes watching her every move.

Flickering candlelight cast dancing phantoms along the aging floorboards. She stepped over and blew out the candles.

Hastily, she gathered her belongings, removed her apron, and slid on her jacket. Each step resonated with the tick-tock of an old clock on the wall, its rhythm adding an ominous undertone to the otherwise peaceful environment.

As she walked outside to activate the security alarm and lock the front door, the letter crinkled softly in her pocket. Streetlamps fought a losing battle against the dense fog draping the town, the feeble glow barely making a dent.

An abrupt clatter of metal cans caused her to spin around. A figure limped out of the alley by the historical society building. As they straightened, she noticed the figure wore a black fedora.

The streetlight caught the wink of what appeared to be cigarette smoke.

Was it possible? Theodore? He was the last person she had seen.

As the figure limped out of sight, she tried to shake off her absurd suspicion. Theodore didn't limp. Theodore didn't smoke. Besides, why would the friendly poet be sneaking outside the historical society at this hour?

Then again, he did have a habit of evening wandering.

His connection to the letter was likely nothing. And yet, she wrestled with the idea that he knew more than he let on by his airy dismissal and unconcern.

As the other businesses dimmed their lights, the blossom-scented air took on an enigmatic quality, as if it cradled concealed secrets.

A gusty breeze tousled the awning of Emma's bakery. The chill seeped through Olivia's thin jacket as she headed to her apartment on Mistwood Lane.

Uneasy, she quickened her pace, resisting the urge to turn around.

She focused on the majestic outlines of snow-capped mountains in the distance, providing a stunning backdrop. This serene little town was a beautiful setting to call home.

Yet, a shiver traced a delicate path down her spine, refusing to be dismantled.

She scolded herself, banishing the urge to cower.

This was a perfect town.

Perhaps too perfect.

Read the rest of Olivia and Daniel's Story.

Pick up your copy of

Whispers of Love in Sweetwater Springs today!
FREE on Kindle Unlimited.

*** End of excerpt *Whispers of Love in Sweetwater Springs*
by Josie Riviera
Copyright © 2024 Josie Riviera
***

Also coming soon:
The Sweetwater Springs Series.

ABOUT THE AUTHOR

Josie Riviera is a *USA TODAY* bestselling author of contemporary, inspirational, and historical sweet romances that read like Hallmark movies. She lives in the Charlotte, NC, area with her wonderfully supportive husband. They share their home with an adorable shih tzu, who constantly needs grooming, and live in an old house forever needing renovations.

To receive my Newsletter and your free sweet romance novella ebook as a thank you gift, sign up HERE.

Become a member of my Read and Review VIP Facebook group for exclusive giveaways and ARCs.

ALSO BY JOSIE RIVIERA

Seeking Patience

Seeking Catherine (always Free!)

Seeking Fortune

Seeking Charity

Seeking Rachel

The Seeking Series

Oh Danny Boy

I Love You More

A Snowy White Christmas

A Portuguese Christmas

Holiday Hearts Book Bundle Volume One

Holiday Hearts Book Bundle Volume Two

Holiday Hearts Book Bundle Volume Three

Holiday Hearts Book Bundle Volume Four

Holiday Hearts Book Bundle Volume Five

Candleglow and Mistletoe

Maeve (Perfect Match)

A Christmas To Cherish

A Love Song To Cherish

A Valentine To Cherish

A Christmas Puppy To Cherish

A Homecoming To Cherish

Romance Stories To Cherish

Aloha to Love

Sweet Peppermint Kisses

Valentine Hearts Boxed Set

1-800-CUPID

1-800-CHRISTMAS

1-800-IRELAND

1-800-SUMMER

1-800-NEW YEAR

The 1-800-Series Sweet Contemporary Romance Bundle

Irish Hearts Sweet Romance Bundle

Holly's Gift

A Chocolate-Box Valentine

A Chocolate-Box Christmas

A Chocolate-Box New Years

A Chocolate-Box Summer Breeze

A Chocolate-Box Christmas Wish

A Chocolate-Box Irish Wedding

Chocolate-Box Hearts

Chocolate-Box Hearts Volume Two

Chocolate-Box Double Hearts

Recipes from the Heart

Leading Hearts

New Year Hearts

SENIOR HEARTS

A Summer To Cherish

Summer Hearts

Romance Stories To Cherish Volume Two

Cherished Hearts

Christmas in the Air

A Very Christian Christmas

The 1-800-Series Volume Two

Christmas Tails of the Heart

Cocoa's Christmas Love

Pawfect Christmas Hearts

Pink Coral Island

Whispers of Love in Sweetwater Springs

Whispers of Maple Memories in Sweetwater Springs

Whispers of Holiday Magic in Sweetwater Springs

Most books are available in ebook, audiobook, paperback, Large Print paperback and Hardcover.

Many are FREE on Kindle Unlimited.

www.ingramcontent.com/pod-product-compliance
Lightning Source LLC
Chambersburg PA
CBHW020837260626
47169CB00003B/1029